I0719334

ONE NIGHT OF LOVE

Print ISBN 978-1-949396-01-0
eISBN 978-1-949396-00-3
Editor: Heather L. Bosch
Cover Artist: Natasha Snow
www.NatashaSnowdesigns.com

Published in the United States of America
Blooming Cactus Publishing LLC
PO Box 131
Wellborn, Texas 77881
www.bloomingcactuspublishing.com

This book is a work of fiction. While reference might be made to actual historical events or existing locations, the names, characters, places and incidents are either the product of the author's imagination or are used fictitiously, and any resemblance to actual persons, living or dead, business establishments, events, or locales is entirely coincidental.

<u>Warning</u>
This e-book contains sexually explicit scenes and adult language and may be considered offensive to some readers. This spicy division of Blooming Cactus Publishing, LLC's e-books are for sale to adults ONLY, as defined by the laws of the country in which you made your purchase. Please store your files wisely, where they cannot be accessed by under-aged readers.

★ ★ ★

DISCLAIMER: Please do not try any new sexual practice, without the guidance of an experienced practitioner. Neither Blooming Cactus Publishing LLC nor its authors will be responsible for any loss, harm, injury or death resulting from use of the information contained in any of its titles.

one night
of
love

ANNA LORES

Blooming Cactus Publishing

To bets and best friends.

ACKNOWLEGMENTS

Writing doesn't happen in my life without the understanding support of my husband and children. Thank you for pitching in, accepting my moments of silence for what they are—me being lost in another world I've created—and loving me for who I am. Thank you to my anonymous beta readers who like to stay on the down low. I love you! I'd like to thank Denise L. for faithfully nudging me every chance she got to submit this story for publication. Thank you to my fabulous editor, Heather Bosch. I'm thrilled you believed in this story and its potential. Your suggestions and edits have made this novel sparkle.

Chapter One

Standing in front of the chest-nut-framed full-length mirror near her hotel room door, Lainie Ivanovski forced her trembling hands to tug the top of her slinky black dress down to show off a little more of her full breasts.

"I can do this." She shook her head. "No. I can't."

She pulled her top back up higher than it was originally and glanced around her wolf-themed room.

The three-star Midnight Howl Hotel hidden just off the Vegas Strip took their motif to heart. Her room reminded her of a stylized wolf's den, from the bison rugs littering the walnut-planked floors to the dark cinnamon walls to the mahogany sleigh bed dressed in bronze linens. On the ceiling above the bed, a mosaic of an enormous black wolf with green eyes howling at a pale yellow moon, which she'd grown to love over the last week, gave her an odd sense of comfort. She would miss the room, the hotel, and the vibrancy everyone around her exuded.

She came to the hotel for a reason. One she

couldn't back out of because it was wrong. If she was successful, she might just have a reason for her husband to keep fighting. *I have to do this. No one will ever know.*

She already knew the man she would approach. He'd been at the hotel bar every night for the past week. They'd exchanged glances, but neither had approached the other. If he didn't take the bait and make the first move, she would approach him for a wild night of sex.

She turned back to the mirror and pulled down the fabric at her bosom to show the edge of lace on her bra.

"One night to make a baby, Mr. Blue Eyes. I'll be gone in the morning." *No commitments. No contact. No complications.*

She pivoted. Her legs weakened, joining her hands in their defiance to move forward with her plan.

She clutched her purse and swallowed the guilty lump in her throat down far enough to keep going.

"I can do this."

She pulled off her wedding ring and slipped it into the zipper pouch in her purse. *No one will ever know.*

Grasping at the barest remnants of confidence, she rubbed her hands together to stop trembling. She closed her hand around the doorknob and twisted.

One night is all I need. Just one night.

The stroll down the dimly lit sky-blue hallway to the hotel bar seemed like a death march, not a new beginning. *This is hopeless. I want a baby. I want to bring some hope into…*

"You look great," Henrietta, the concierge, said, magically appearing beside her.

"You move so fast," Lainie said, picking up Henrietta's brisk pace down the hall toward the Moonlight Lobby.

Henrietta coughed a laugh. "I'm one of the slower ones here. Are you gambling tonight?"

"No, it's been a long five days of intense classes. I thought I'd wind down at the bar. I might go for a midnight walk through the cactus garden." A part of her didn't want to leave the desert and go back to reality in the humid South.

"Your room is vacant until Monday night. Are you sure you don't want to extend and stay through the weekend? I'll give you a great deal."

"I'll let you know if I need another night." She didn't want to prolong her visit, but she would if she wasn't successful in seducing the gorgeous man.

Hope he's willing to forget contraception and let it fly. Shit. I need to ask him about diseases. I should ask him for his doctor's number for verification. Maybe he could open his patient portal on the Internet and show me his clean bill of health. I hope he has one. Shit.

"How about I just set it up, and if you leave early, that's okay? I know there's an extra massage course offered, which ends Sunday night. I could call and sign you up last minute. The instructor has room for you." Henrietta put her arm around Lainie. "You know you want to stay. I promise to kick you out on Monday."

I might need tomorrow. If he can't prove he's healthy, then I've got to find someone else. I'm freaking ovulating. Right now.

"Uh." *I don't know.* "Okay. Sign me up for the

class."

"Great." Henrietta's quick grin seemed as if she was mischievously helping with Lainie's plan to get pregnant. "I'll leave an itinerary under your door. Class starts at noon tomorrow, so have a great night and sleep in."

Lainie stood at the entrance to the Bitten by a Wolf Bar with Henrietta. She gazed and was transfixed at the sign above the door. *Once I go in, there is no backing out.*

"It's just the name. No one's actually been bitten by a wolf inside the bar and told me about it." Henrietta patted her on the back, opened the tinted glass door, and seemed to offer an encouraging nudge forward. "You look like you could be the wolf ready to bite. I should give the guys a warning about you tonight."

Lainie's heart fluttered at the ridiculousness of Henrietta's motivational words. She slammed her hands against her chest over her rapidly beating heart. *I probably look more like a lamb going to slaughter.*

Henrietta's eyes narrowed. "Relax. I was just kidding. That was my way of saying you look really good and need to be careful."

"Oh. Yeah. I know. I was just…" She tamped down the anxiety creeping through her body like tendrils of poison ivy. "Sorry. I'm not used to being complimented. I don't usually dress like this, but if I can't dress like this here in Vegas, I can't dress like this anywhere."

Henrietta looked her up and down. "You can dress like that in any state in the Union with the right man. You just need to find that man."

I found the right man. He… Don't go there.

"Thanks. Tonight, I'd just like to have some fun. I'm hoping I might even get asked to dance."

"Between you and me…" Henrietta lowered her voice and drew closer. "Most of these guys are looking for one-night stands, not forever. You're a forever kind of catch. Keep your eyes open, and be safe."

"I'm not looking for forever. A dance or two would be nice." *And a healthy man with blue eyes and a high sperm count.*

"All you have to do is tell them you're the great Lainie of Atlanta, massage therapist to the stars," Henrietta said.

Lainie shook her head in a panic. "No, no, no, no. I don't want anyone to know who I am. Please don't tell anyone."

Henrietta lifted her pinched fingers to her lips and drew them across as she closed her mouth. "Lips are zipped."

Taking in a deep breath, Lainie glanced around the bar she hadn't realized she'd entered. *Where is everyone?*

With a little nudge from her new friend, she stepped up to the bar counter. The man behind the counter hadn't been there all week. She would have remembered the Celtic warrior with chocolate eyes and an athlete's body. If he had blue eyes, she would consider making a baby with him. He had to be healthy. She crossed her legs and squeezed them together to stop the flow of juices from her pussy.

"Neal, my friend Lainie needs a drink," Henrietta said. "Give her the house special to start the night, and keep an eye on her for me."

"Will do, Hen." Neal's deep voice traveled over Lainie's flesh like molasses, thick and sweet.

If only you had blue eyes. She looked down at his left hand. *And weren't married. You would be perfect.*

In the blink of an eye, Neal mixed up and placed a frothy red drink down in front of her.

"Here's a Howling Dog. Enjoy."

"Howling Dog, huh?" She moved her head from side to side, contemplating whether to drink it or not. She leaned forward, her breasts pressing against the edge of the bar.

The first drink for courage and however many more it takes to loosen up.

"Well, take a sip, and tell me if you like it." Neal licked his lips as his gaze drifted to her chest.

She stared at his mouth. His tongue peeked out and caressed the length of his succulent lips. Her belly quivered with a new sensation. *Maybe eye color doesn't matter.*

She lifted the glass to her lips. A heavy haze seemed to settle over her like midnight fog over a swamp. Struggling for clarity, she followed her desires and sipped the drink.

"Delicious." She sighed. Sweet raspberry and tart lemon challenged her taste buds for control. "Howling Dog makes me want to howl like a wolf."

A strange growling noise released from his mouth, making her all warm and tingly.

"Thanks. So, what brings you to Vegas?"

"I took a class for work." She took another sip, nearly finishing the sweet raspberry cocktail. "Henrietta is signing me up for another, but I don't think I'll stay. I really need to get home."

He mixed her another drink in a shaker. "*Stay the weekend.*"

The room seemed to heat up a few degrees. *I want him. God, what is wrong with me? He's married.*

He poured the raspberry liquid into her glass, filling it to the top.

"Did I drink all that already?" She gazed up into his eyes for validation.

"You sure did. And looked good doing it."

She pressed her hand to her chest. His gaze followed her fingers as she pushed the edge of the fabric down, revealing more of her flesh.

"A little more," Neal whispered. "We like seeing skin."

Her lips parted on a whisper. "Really?"

She slid the top down farther, staring at his encouraging eyes.

"Really. A little more. This is an adult bar. Women come in here with pasties and panties Friday and Saturday nights. You're overdressed for this bar tonight, and I, for one, love seeing a beautiful woman showing off what God gave her."

She sucked down the last of the drink. Could she seduce a man? Every woman she'd encountered in the week she'd been in Vegas had been beautiful. *Am I pretty enough?*

With both hands at her cleavage, she pulled the neckline of her dress down, showing him the very tip of her areola. "This much?"

He pushed a shot of clear liquid toward her. "Drink it, and show me a little more."

She hadn't let out the wild in her since before she met her husband, but tonight she needed to access a little of her roots. No thinking. No rules. Nothing was stopping her from getting pregnant.

She picked up the shot glass and gulped, accepting the familiar burn of her preferred liquid. *Just tonight. Only tonight.*

Neal exhaled. "You're my kind of girl. My wife will be here soon. We like to play."

He placed his large hands over her fingers at her chest.

"Show me the rest of your breasts." He licked his lips. "Then, lift your top just past your nipples. Push your chest toward me. I'll do it for you."

Without thinking, she straightened her back and pushed out her chest. "Please, sir."

His confident hands traveled along hers, up her arms to her shoulders, and headed down over her bare skin to the fabric of her blouse. "Your skin is so smooth and soft."

"Thank you, sir," she exhaled in a breathy voice she hadn't heard since she walked away from the Dominant/submissive lifestyle for her husband. It had been so long since her husband felt good enough to take care of her. So long since he had the energy to make love to her. She was going to change that when she went back. She had to. At least for one night.

He pulled the fabric under her black lace demi bra. He lifted her breasts from the cups.

"You need rings in these. Get them now." He pinched her right nipple.

She gasped as heat spread from her pussy and belly to both her nipples. She arched her back, offering more of her breasts to him. "Yes, sir."

"Go to the back of the bar, and enter the Sparkling Collar room. My wife will pierce you for free."

"Yes, sir." She slid off the bar stool and walked with a swing in her step over the empty dance floor. Spotting a large gold-glittered collar and leash painted on a door, she quickly moved toward it.

CHAPTER TWO

THE DOOR TO THE SPARKLING Collar boutique opened as she lifted her hand to knock.

A slender woman about her age with pink short hair, a strip of white sheer fabric over her breasts, and a piece of string wrapped around her hips with a triangle of gold in the shape of a penis dangling over her mons stepped forward.

"Come in, Lainie."

Lainie blinked. *How do you know my name? How did you know I was coming?*

Her feet moved over the threshold as her brain stayed in a growing haze.

"Pretty breasts deserve pretty jewelry," the woman said, guiding her to the middle of the small boutique filled with jewelry, clothing, and lingerie. "Let me see what the rest of your sexy body looks like. Undress."

With the help of the woman, Lainie removed her dress.

"Much better, isn't it?" the woman asked.

"Yes, ma'am." She hadn't felt this alive in…*ever.*

She widened her stance as the woman walked in

a circle inspecting her. *I miss this. I miss being around women comfortable in their own skin. I miss men like Neal.*

"You're too beautiful to be covered up. I think we're going to be best friends." The woman's small hands slid like the caress of a lover along Lainie's back. Continuing her inspection, the assertive nature of the woman made Lainie give over more control.

"Mmm," the woman moaned. "Your scent is *enchanting.*"

"Thank you, ma'am."

"Safe, sane, and consensual is what we're all about here at the Midnight Howl Hotel. Are you familiar with the terms 'Dominant' and 'submissive'?"

"Yes, ma'am. Are the men that come here into that kind of lifestyle?" Juices trickled from her pussy, wetting her inner thighs.

"Yes. All the men are here to find a sweet little sub to fuck. 'Red' is the safe word. Did you sign the consent form? Fill out the hard and soft limit form?"

"Um. I haven't signed anything yet." *As long as it means getting Blue Eyes and fucking, I'll sign anything you want.*

Her hand slid over Lainie's mons.

"So pretty and smooth." Fingers dipped between her folds.

Lainie's pulse raced. *Will she finger fuck me? Lick me? A ménage with you and Neal would start the night off right. I'd go find Blue Eyes and then kneel at his feet. He'd order me onto my hands and knees. Mount me from behind and fuck me over and over and over again.*

"I'll sign anything you need." *Just hurry.*

Thin fingers dipped into Lainie's pussy.

"Oh, yes," Lainie moaned.

"I want you to get what you need tonight," Neal whispered into her ear from behind her. His bare front pressed against her back. "Sophia, get the tablet. Go over the form with her, so she can sign it. Then I'll give it to Danny at the bar."

"Yes, sir," Sophia said, slipping her fingers from Lainie's pussy. She licked them clean as she seemed to swiftly float over the wood floor like a surfer would a wave and disappeared behind a black curtain like she was going into an underwater tunnel.

"I made this just for you." Neal's lips rubbed against her ear. "It's up to you if you want to drink it."

He massaged along her ribs under her breasts. "You're giving off the most alluring scent. With every second, you become more irresistible."

"I'll have it after I sign." She slid her hands between her back and his bare front. "Are you wearing clothes?"

"Clothing is optional on Friday nights at Bitten by a Wolf Bar." He shifted. His hard cock rubbed against her ass. His hands drifted to her breasts, cupping them firmly.

Closing her eyes, she relaxed against him.

"I want to fuck a man with blue eyes. I want him bare and his cum to be all over me and inside me, but I want to fuck you too. I want Sophia to suck and lick my clit. I want my pussy swollen and satisfied by the end of the night."

"Raise your hands only if you're ready for your nipples to be pierced."

She raised her hands. She'd always liked the sharp

prick of a needle, the rush of blood, and the heat and desire that came afterward. Nothing turned her on like her husband biting her shoulder when he climaxed. She shuddered.

"Do you want to watch?" Neal asked.

She shook her head. She'd been through it before, but she'd let the holes close up after she left her Dom for her husband.

"Breathe in," Sophia said. "Exhale."

Neal's tongue dipped into her ear as the sting of the needle slid through her nipple.

"Uhn." She gasped. Her breast throbbed. Fire burst from her heart, rushing to her breast.

"Exhale," Sophia said.

Lainie's chest constricted. She forced air from her lungs as the needle pierced the other nipple. "Shit, that hurt."

"I had to make a new hole. The old one wasn't in a good spot."

Lainie opened her eyes to Sophia's amber gaze. "How do they look?"

Sophia's lips pressed against hers. "Lovely. Like you."

"Thank you," Lainie said.

Thick fingers separated her pussy folds and circled the ring in her clit. "Sweet pussy."

"Thank you, sir."

Sophia sighed. "Double penetration? Light bondage? Heavy bondage? What's your pain threshold?" Her lips brushed against Lainie's neck as she asked hard and soft limits.

As Lainie answered each question, her needs became clearer. Her words became bolder. With a man like Neal holding her, worries seemed to vanish. She lifted her finger and then signed her name on the screen.

"We've closed off the entrance to outsiders," Neal whispered.

She angled her head to the side, offering her neck. Her head swam as the most exquisite scent of man and woods saturated the air around her. "Thank you."

He leaned forward. His lips were millimeters from hers. "You're a queen, Lainie. Every man wants to dominate you, and every woman wants to serve you."

"I want to be dominated." *Dominated by someone worthy. Someone I can give over all my burdens to. Someone I can leave in the morning.*

"No, you *need* to be dominated." His lips touched hers. "Ready?"

"I need a drink." *That scent. That man. I want that man. Woods and marigolds.*

"I've got a fresh one," Sophia said, handing her another goblet filled with what looked like the house special. "This one has a special healing herb mixture."

"Thank you." Lainie sipped the drink, tasting the same raspberry and tart lemon as before. "I can't leave the bar naked."

"I'll make sure you're covered before you leave," Neal said. His firm hands held her hips.

Soft hands caressed her thighs. A wonderful wet tongue licked along her folds.

Lainie gazed between her legs. Exquisite caramel eyes met her gaze. Her legs shook as the skilled tongue circled her clit ring. Around and around Sophia licked.

"Sophia," Lainie moaned. She rocked her hips as Sophia poured the foundation of pleasure for the rest of the night.

"Drink." Neal groaned.

Lainie drank as she heard a rip of foil.

His hard, slick cock pushed at her dark passage.

"Neal. Sophia." Lainie's knees weakened.

"Need to fuck you," Neal rumbled. He adjusted his cock to her pussy. "I'm going to—"

"Neal," a man shouted. "Not your pussy to fuck."

Neal stopped immediately.

The warrior's body supporting her disappeared in a flash.

She fell backward and landed on her ass.

"Shit," the man said.

She turned her head toward his voice and immediately recognized him—the man with blue eyes—but he wasn't alone. He was one among a group of seven gorgeous men. The largest of them stood in the center.

The one she had earlier hoped would approach her made no effort to help her up. He kept his place in line next to the man in the center who appeared to be the leader.

Dazed from the fall, she sat in place and watched as the blue-eyed gaze so much like her husband's scanned her over not like a lover, but more like a doctor searching for any anomalies or disease.

He shifted his gaze to the big sexy man in the middle.

Following his gaze, she turned her attention to the man with green eyes, the tallest, broadest, and strongest one. The leader.

"Oh God, I want you," she unintentionally

voiced her thoughts.

The man she couldn't take her eyes off strode to her. His nostrils flared, and his green eyes seemed to read the sad stories hidden inside her soul—the sadness that compelled her to take this trip, to flirt with blue eyes, and to believe in a miracle.

He reached for her and helped her up.

Something sparked in her blood at his touch. Something that demanded her attention. Something so intense she didn't know what to say, do, or think. Something that shot adrenaline into her blood, pushing at her to run away from him. Something that also told her to crawl into his arms for protection, for comfort.

"Would you like to dance?" His deep voice cut right to her pussy, making it throb.

Unable to turn away from him or ignore his question, she stuttered, "I-I… Y-yes, s-sir." So much for being the seductress. Her lips parted, yet no additional words came to her brain or through her mouth. She wobbled as she stood on bare feet and was unable to unlock her focus on him.

"Your name is Lainie?" the man asked. His nostrils flared again, more subtly than the last time.

She was glad she stood so close to him. The excitement between her thighs at the man's touch produced such need that the flow of cream moved steadily down her thighs. *You. Me. Baby.*

"Lainie, I'm Luke."

He guided her away from the boutique and onto the dance floor where a small gathering of couples bumped and ground to the lazy beat of a blues song.

"Dance with me," he whispered.

Lainie slid her hands up his athletic chest to the broad shoulders she would bite when he made her come and latched her fingers together behind his neck. Her hands barely reached, but he took control, guiding her forward and onto the tips of her toes. He pulled her tightly against his chest.

"Why are you here?" She was glad her brain decided to complete a sentence while she tried to remember the list of things to ask him, which at the moment eluded her. "You don't have blue eyes. Damn it."

Maybe there are blue eyes in your family.

"I'm here to meet you." He dragged his lips over her cheek. "Danny told me about you. He's the one you've been staring at all week. I would have come earlier, but I just got back in town today."

She gazed at his handsome face, mesmerized.

"I'm not sure I know who you mean." She knew exactly who he meant. But she couldn't believe the blue-eyed man spoke of her to his friends or that the man holding her came to the bar tonight hoping to see her.

"Danny is the one at the bar mixing you another drink." He pivoted her to face the bar.

The man she'd planned to make a baby with lifted a glass filled with a Howling Dog special and smiled.

"Oh." She cleared her throat. "*Him.*"

Luke's eyes sparkled with the beginnings of a pearly white grin. "Yeah. *Him.*"

He lifted his arm and turned her in a tight twirl back to face him.

"He likes you, but I'm your perfect match."

Her gaze darted from Luke to the exit several

times. *I should go.*

She breathed in, and with it, Luke's intoxicating woodsy scent filled her lungs, melting her reservations and enforcing sudden and unwanted intense feelings of love. *Nothing will make me leave you.*

Waves of heat like the Sahara radiated from him. And she wanted more. So. Much. More.

She tilted her head up, closed her eyes, parted her lips, and readied for his kiss. "Do you feel that?" she asked.

"Yes." Luke's hands traveled down her back to her ass with lightning speed. "Is the blue-eyes-only rule a hard limit?"

What? Blue eyes? "Huh?"

"Is the blue-eyes-only rule a hard limit? I plan on fucking you and giving you every ounce of my cum when I do it."

She moaned. "I'm not normally like this."

"You're in he—" He cleared his throat. "You're so hot, Lainie. Are blue eyes a hard limit?"

"You have the most beautiful green eyes." She leaned in and nuzzled her face against his neck. "I have no hard limits with you."

"Son of a…" He shifted his weight, wrapped his hands around her thighs, and lifted her up.

"You smell so good." She curled her legs around his narrow waist. "You're wearing too many clothes. They itch."

"How old are you?" He reached between her legs and removed his brown leather belt.

"Twenty-eight."

"Do you like your age?"

She nodded. She loved being twenty-eight, but she was looking forward to being pregnant and twenty-nine. Maybe she'd get lucky, and her blue eyes would be the dominant gene.

"I'm taking you back to my room," he said.

CHAPTER THREE

LAINIE'S WISH WAS COMING TRUE. *A sexy, strong man. No questions. No expectations. One night of wild sex. Never see each other again.*

She rubbed her nose along his collarbone to the notch at the center. *Sun and sand. Cactus blooms. Are you wearing cologne?*

His biceps bulged, and a deliciously deep noise sounding like a rumble of thunder vibrated from him.

She shuddered with pleasure as the sound from him rocked her to the core. Confidence filled her as Luke cradled her in his arms and strode over the threshold of the stark-white Howling Honeymoon room.

He heeled off his sneakers and kicked the door closed. He moved silently and swiftly across the white carpet, stopping next to the side of the white-washed four-poster canopy bed. Heavy white lace panels hung from the canopy, shielding the interior from the rest of the room.

"I've waited my entire life for you," he said as she slid down his hard body.

"I'm here for one night." *I can't stay longer. I'm needed at home.*

He parted the center lace panel at the side of the king-size bed. He pulled it open and then wrapped the lace around the headboard post. A white lace duvet with an embroidered rendering of a black wolf howling at a yellow moon covered the mattress.

Privacy. Peace. A place to call home. "I love that picture."

A low, approving rumble vibrated from him. "Undress me."

A light sheen of perspiration slicked her skin. Her hands trembled, making contact with his black-and-green cotton T-shirt. A zing of electricity slithered through her, strangely steadying her and compelling her to keep going. She pushed the hem of his shirt up over his defined abdomen.

"You're magnificent," she whispered. *Perfect. Healthy. Handsome.*

She continued lifting the soft fabric past a broad chest built for heavyweight boxing. Instincts took over, and she placed a soft kiss over his heart. *Mine.*

He rounded his shoulders and reached forward as she pulled off the shirt. His arms dropped down like a curtain around her, closing her in a private cocoon. His hand slid to her hips as he ground his large erection into her belly.

She pressed another soft kiss to his bare chest. Kissing his mouth would be a mistake. She couldn't get that close, risk the emotions, the guilt, or the chance of falling for him even more. She had to stop the growing carnal desire to experience the intimacy of his lips on hers, of his taste on her tongue, or of anything that would make her contact him again.

She rubbed her nose along the center of his chest, darting her tongue over his tanned skin and sneaking a taste of woods and sun.

She journeyed downward, exploring the ridges and valleys of his ribs and defined abs, nuzzling, kissing, and licking her way to the dusting of dark hair beneath his navel leading to her prize.

Closing her eyes, she imagined a forest surrounding them—his scent, his strength, and his love protecting her from harm. She would never feel alone with him. He would always be there. He wouldn't wither away before her eyes. He wouldn't…

He gasped as her fingers caressed his waist along the rim of his jeans.

She unbuttoned his jeans and dropped to her knees, her thighs spread wide, chest arched, and hands desperate to uncover the part that would give her everything she ever wanted.

The tines of metal lowered, his zipper gave way, and she peeled his pants from his powerful thighs. One leg lifted and then the other as she removed the fabric from under his feet.

Her face connected with hard, hot flesh. She opened her eyes, finding his cock exactly where she wanted it—in front of her mouth.

Up and down, she brushed against his hard length with her lips, her cheek, and her nose. "May I suck?"

He cupped her face. He inhaled and exhaled in rhythm with her labored breathing. "Lick."

His erection seemed to grow longer, and the

veins bulged.

She shuddered. Her pussy quivered, wanting the void filled, but it was her mouth that salivated for the first taste.

Her moist tongue slid from the base of his thick shaft up to the wide head and lapped a gift of pearly liquid from the weeping eye. The taste of salty man, juniper, and marigold exploded in her mouth. She parted her hungry lips and covered the head of his cock.

He firmly gripped her hair like a ponytail and then pulled her head back. "No."

She swallowed. Only a drop of his succulent seed entered her system.

Without warning, he lifted her up and playfully tossed her onto the bed.

"I want to be inside you." Luke growled like a wild animal about to eat its prey. "I can't wait any longer."

She bounced on the middle of the mattress as he stalked her. No Dom she'd ever been with was as confident and powerful as the man prepared to dominate her. Something she didn't understand came over her. She stared straight into his emerald eyes, challenging his authority over her.

The warning in his glare seemed to accept her test, giving her no doubt he would subdue her and showing her he was worthy to create a life with her. She scrambled off the bed. The desire to be chased by him and claimed by him overwhelmed her.

Within two steps, he caught her. He wrapped his arms around her, pulled her back to his front, and squeezed.

"My naughty girl needs to remember I am in charge." The rumble that left his chest seemed to vibrate her already sensitive clit. "Get on the bed."

She wiggled to get out of his hold. "I'm trying to get on the bed, sir."

He groaned. "Try harder."

Swinging her hips and shoulders, she pivoted inside his hold. She averted her gaze from his. "Better?"

"Much." His arms relaxed. "Bed, now. I'm going to reward you."

She pulled down the linens to the foot of the bed and climbed up, getting on her hands and knees. Ready and waiting, her sex pulsed and throbbed in anticipation of his next move.

Get up here, and do it. Fuck me. Please, fuck me.

Shivers blew over her hot flesh from her limbs to her belly as she imagined making love to him—making a baby with him.

Luke flipped her over. He seemed possessive as he crawled over her body.

He nudged her legs apart and settled between them. He hovered over her. Face-to-face. Lips millimeters apart.

"Your life is going to change after this."

You have no idea how true that is. You're the key to getting my miracle. You're going to save and make a life tonight.

"You're mine," he whispered. "All mine."

Only for tonight, Luke. Only for tonight.

CHAPTER FOUR

LUKE STRUGGLED TO TAKE HIS time enter-ing her sweet pussy. He wanted to dive in and keep going deeper, deeper, and deeper until he found her mating spot, but he couldn't hurt her like that. She was tight. So tight. Too tight. Way too tight.

She couldn't have had sex in months. Maybe years.

He rarely went a week without it. A healthy sex life made waiting for a mate more manageable.

Traditionally, werewolves emitted a mating scent as soon as both partners' wolves were matured. No matter where in the world they were, the scent would travel, and the more powerful of the two went on a search for the other. A pack mate would be assigned to accompany the werewolf to help track the mate's location and then witness the cer-emony.

But Lainie was different.

Being a human compatible with a werewolf was rare. So rare that he'd only heard of it hap-pening twice in the past five hundred years.

Having a human go through a werewolf's mating heat before turning was even rarer. And a human searching for her forever mate, suffering through a werewolf heat before turning, and being born with a DNA indicator that activated when she arrived within in a hundred miles of his home was the rarest kind. And she was that human. His human. His mate. His lover. His wife. And she would turn into a werewolf as soon as the next full moon appeared.

He wanted tonight to be perfect. He'd planned to wine and dine her and to fall in love more organically, not take her back to his room and claim her first. But Neal was on bar duty tonight, smelled her mating heat, and had to show her his goods like a horny teen. The man nearly fucked everything up by touching her. Hell, her sexy scent had everyone in the hotel on edge all week.

Werewolves from all over Vegas booked rooms to see if they were the one she was looking for.

They weren't.

He was.

She couldn't have known why she kept going back to the bar night after night. Instincts would have guided her actions and her thoughts as she waited for him to find her. She couldn't have remembered Danny finding her pacing back and forth in the classic mating trance in the bar or taking her back to her room and tucking her into bed. But fate had been on Luke's side.

Danny had smelled her luscious aroma. And once in her presence, he had recognized her as Luke's mate and understood the extraordinary circumstances—her human status, the rise of her werewolf heat, and the need to protect her until Luke came home to mate her. He immediately called Luke for instructions on how to proceed.

Honoring Luke's requests to follow the old ways of his family pack traditions, Danny had the sheets in her bedroom changed to ones Luke had slept on. To lessen the anxiety of not finding her mate, Danny wore Luke's clothes for all their interactions at the hotel bar during the week, until Luke got home from meeting with the World Alpha in Germany. Allowing her to breathe in her mate's scent through his clothes the rest of the week at the bar, she had quickly relaxed, sat down, had a drink, and stared at him for hours until it was time to help her back to her room for another night alone. It had been the most excruciating week, trying to get back to Vegas from an Alpha conference in Germany to meet her before she left his territory, but he did it. Fate brought him his forever mate, perfect in every way.

"More. Deeper." She moaned into his mouth. She stroked her needy tongue against his in a dance of control and desire. She tilted her hips, giving him the entrance he needed to mate her.

"I'm trying to keep from hurting you. I'm larger than most." He thrust into her a little deeper with more force, holding back from unleashing his beast.

"Damn it, I don't care if it hurts. I'm going to die if you don't get your cock embedded inside me." Lainie bent her left knee and dug her heel into the bed, giving him more leverage to thrust deeper.

Thank you, mate. I can't wait to meet your beautiful beast once she emerges.

He pulled her right leg down and wrapped it around his waist. He abandoned her lips and grabbed the post closest to him on the bed.

"Lainie." He growled, allowing his wolf to rise closer to the surface. He wouldn't let his beast take over, not until she turned.

"I can take it. Please," she begged. "Go deeper. Harder. However you want. I want it all."

"Oh fuck, yes." He grunted. *Your beast will rival the strongest female Alphas. You are mine.*

His legs coiled. He shouldn't go deeper yet. He'd hurt her. He'd risk ripping her…

"Do it," she screamed. "The heat. I'm so hot."

Releasing his power, he thrust forward. His cock drove so deeply inside her that the edge of his balls slid in too.

"Oh God," she gasped. "It hurts."

The first night together rarely produced a baby. But he was the Alpha and ready to have a family. He'd been waiting for her all these years for his mate. Maybe, with the right…

He sucked in as the head of his cock extended for the first time, confirming she was the one—the only one perfectly made for him.

Her pussy molded around him, trapping his cock in the mating niche for the duration of the ceremony.

"Fuck, yes." He and his beast accepted her, and she accepted them.

He howled as excruciating pain poured through his veins. His cock extended farther, tunneling into her.

"Shit." His beast warred to gain control. The wolf inside him wanted out. Wanted her. Wanted…

Tears pricked at his eyes. His cock stretched as her pussy seemed to twist the head of his cock like tourniquet, cutting off the bottom but saving the top.

He ground his teeth and glared down at her. "Stop that."

"Oh, Luke." She sighed. Her face relaxed with a smile on her lips. "I love you."

Her pussy released the pressure on his cock but held him in her warm cave. The pain subsided, and a pleasure he'd never experienced entered instead.

I'm finally mated. Danny found my mate. My dick is going to hang down to my fucking knees the way she yanked it. He grinned. *Hell yeah, it will. All she needs to do is milk my cock and...*

"God, yes." She moaned as she rolled her hips.

He had to stay still. She'd taken him into her mating place, and it was his job to stay there until his DNA mixed with hers so his scent would forever be on her. Any wolf who met her would know she was his. The bites were next. His wolf would come forward enough to bite her, mark her, and claim her. Every wolf would see her sparkling silver mating marks. She would change from being a human with a werewolf compatibility gene to a full-fledged, changing at least once a month into a werewolf for eternity.

The far-off look in her blue eyes held the classic mating trance—running on instincts and heart and body taking what it needed. His trance would come but only after he'd completed his job.

Her pussy rippled, milking his cock and squeezing so hard that he stopped breathing. Her fingers dug into his hips.

The middle of his shaft stretched and bounced back like a yo-yo as she rocked her hips.

"Oh God. Oh God. Lift my hips. Keep them up." Perspiration trickled down her face and neck. The trance seemed to continue as she babbled, moaned, and writhed.

He held her, trying to keep her from dislodging him before the mating was finished. "Slow down, baby. Slow down."

"Please. Please. Please." She panted each word. Her face scrunched, revealing what seemed like soulful desperation and pain mixed with intense pleasure.

He'd never seen a woman do that during a mating. *Must be the human DNA changing.*

"I cleared the hotel," Danny said. "Damn, you two are still in the mating hold?"

He hadn't heard Danny enter. *Was I in a trance? No. I would know. I'm the Alpha.*

He turned his head and stared at his friend and Beta. "How long have you been here?"

"Just got back. I stayed to witness the mating. Then I set up the timer. Neal got his shit together enough to relieve me at the bar. I just got back." Danny glanced behind him, then back at Luke. "Four hours. You were in a heavy trance for most of it."

I was?

Lainie stopped moving under him and sighed.

"Your dick is going to hurt like hell."

"Worth it," he said. He held her legs still and rolled until she was on top of him. He bent his knees and placed his feet flat on the bed.

She snuggled atop him with her sweet mouth pressed against his neck. Warm puffs of air blew against his flesh with every sweet, sleepy sigh she released.

"She's going to be good for the girls in the pack," Danny said.

"Yes. She is going to be a unifying force." *Mine.*

Moisture dripped from her pussy onto him. The mating had to be almost completed. Four hours was extreme, even for an Alpha of his caliber.

A light tug on the head of his cock seemed to pull the last of his sperm from his balls. Her vaginal walls relaxed.

She exhaled deeply. A strange scent of smoke and whiskey released from her pores, and then the most delicious scent of peaches, peanuts, and pine took over.

"That was weird," Danny mumbled. "Could she belong to someone else?"

"Doesn't matter. She's mine now."

"Hmm. Luke," she whispered. "So good."

The rhythmic milking of his cock subsided.

"Yes. She's mine." He relaxed his legs and hips. Now it was Danny's job to confirm the mating had been completed. "Nothing left. I'm giving you permission to confirm I now have a mate."

Danny walked over to the bed and took several pictures of them together. He checked the time and documented it. "Do I really have to pull your dick from her?"

"It's part of the ritual, and I can't do it myself. I've done it for damn near everyone mated in the pack, and you'll have to do it when I'm not available. It's an honor, not a chore."

Danny never liked doing anything that might have an emotional link, whether it was being present for a birth, helping with a bitch in heat, or being the witness of a mating. Danny was always decidedly absent.

But, if there was a friend in need of backup during a fight, a woman to fuck, or a pack member needing a tracker to search for their mate, Danny Wedekind stood first in line to help.

His Beta slouched. "I know. I'm not good with this shit."

"Take it slow and breathe. You've got to sniff and lick to confirm we're one hundred percent bonded."

"I don't need to lick to know you two are bonded." Danny slowly withdrew Luke's cock. "Damn. I sure do hope this thing shrinks back to normal, or you won't be able to walk."

"It will. This is why I need you to take care of any emergencies in the pack until the honeymoon is over."

"She's pregnant. I can confirm there's a baby growing inside her." Danny smiled. "Congrats. First time with her. You're a stud."

Luke laughed. "Hell yeah. I'm not the Alpha for nothing."

"I'll send out an announcement to the pack and then the rest of the community on the West Coast. I'll let the East Coast Alpha know about your good news too." Danny took another picture and walked toward the door. "That wasn't so bad."

"See? You need to try some new things. Step outside the box."

Danny opened the door to the living room of the suite.

"Whatever." He glanced back. "Enjoy the rest of your night, stud."

The door closed.

"We're alone, Lainie," he whispered.

She didn't seem to be out of the trance yet. *You should be out of it by now.*

He'd witnessed hundreds of classic werewolf matings over the years, and every single one of them had been finished in less than two hours. Something serious must have happened to her to demand his undivided attention, but maybe it was just the human factor. Whatever the reason, she was his now.

He was her Alpha, her protector, her lover, and her mate, and she was his first priority for the rest of their days on earth.

She pushed up against his chest and sat up. She brushed her layers of brindled brown and golden hair hiding her beautiful face behind her ears. The haze of the mating trance made her ocean-blue eyes sparkle.

"Wow. Can we do that again?"

His cock hardened, and his balls ached to give her exactly what she wanted.

"Yes. I'm going to fuck you—All. Night. Long." *More like all weekend long.*

She stretched her arms over her head and exhaled a slow, sexy moan. "Prove it."

Sassy mate. "Oh, I'll prove it."

She collapsed onto his chest and curled her slender arms around his neck. "Are you saying…?" Her warm, moist breath blew along the curve of his neck leading to his shoulder. "You've got the stamina to do it?"

"Hell, yeah. I do."

Her teeth grazed the edge of his shoulder.

"Don't do that." His beast liked it too much.

"You don't like it?" She pinched his skin with her teeth.

His beast rumbled, and a low growl left his lips. "I said—"

She opened her mouth wide and bit down hard. She rotated her hips and met his cock.

He shuddered.

"Oh fuck." *You're not a wolf. You're not supposed to bite. You're not supposed to…*

She laved over the mark, which would show her claim on him. "You like that?"

"Uhm. Don't do that." *You're going to make me lose control.*

"You smell so good. So clean. So healthy. You taste like the freshness of spring in bloom." She nibbled along his collarbone. "I want more of you."

She exhaled, and the scent of peaches, peanuts, pine along with juniper, marigold, and sand expanded outward. The entire hotel and grounds would be covered in their aroma if it wasn't already.

Teeth cut into the meaty muscle of his shoulder.

"Yes," he roared. *Your wolf is forming.*

A little wolfie growl left her lips. "Mine."

His control shattered.

In a swift motion, he turned her onto her belly and lifted her hips. "I warned you."

"I want the consequences." She wiggled her ass. Her pink pussy glistened with their fluids.

He lifted his cock to her entrance and fed his hunger. In and out of her narrow sheath. His thighs quivered. His hips thrust back and forth. Her warm walls took him into her home, her heart, and her soul.

The beat of her heart rang in his ears, screaming at him to bite into her bones and mark her to the marrow. Her pulse fluttered in the vein in her neck.

Bite her. Taste her. Now.

His teeth lengthened. His beast rose inside him, begging to be let loose, shift, and take his mate.

Her breath labored.

Now. Now. Now. Instincts ran wild. His teeth sank into her porcelain flesh. Down they descended through fascia, muscle, and bone.

Crack.

The taste of peaches, peanuts, and pine inundated his mouth, nostrils, and lungs.

He bucked and drove inside her silky warm center. In and out. Over and over. He gripped her hips, pushed her away, and pulled her back on to his hard cock.

He tore his mouth from her shoulder and bit into her other shoulder. And her neck. And her arms. And her sides. Marking her in the tradition of his family's pack. Claiming every inch of her.

His balls drew up. His dick jerked.

"Luke," she shouted, her voice changing between that of a human and a baby wolf.

His beast clawed to get through his skin to emerge. He threw his head back and gave voice to his wolf.

Triumphant howls spilled from his mouth as cum spurted out of his cock. He squirmed to get deeper as her pussy pulsed in waves around him. Bliss stepped into his heart and placed her inside.

Always by my side, loving me, supporting me. Together for eternity.

He flopped onto his side, pulling her back to his

front. His wolf retreated, happy and satisfied.

For the first time in his life, Luke had everything he ever wanted—a mate, a baby on the way, and peace between the West and East North American Packs.

CHAPTER FIVE

HARDENED MUSCLES FROM YEARS OF working out lay beneath her. Masculine arms made for cuddling gently curled around her. Thick cock that could go all night stood poised at her pussy, ready for another round. *Mmm.*

Lainie barely lifted her lids, but she recognized him under her.

Luke. Incredible lover. Husband-worthy. Father material. Her chest constricted at the thought of leaving him. *He's a good man.*

His hands glided over the curve of her ass and down between her thighs. His fingers curled into her pussy. He half mumbled, half growled something she couldn't make out but seemed happy about.

She definitely had one too many last night, but if this man couldn't get her pregnant, then fate didn't want her to have a baby. Fate didn't want her to have a miracle, to give a gift of happiness to her husband, or to make him fight harder to live.

"Lainie," Luke mumbled in his sleep. "I love you."

His chest rose, lifting her with the powerful

motion.

She carefully rolled off his chest and stopped at his side. She stayed frozen and tucked between the side of his chest and his arm as he exhaled a soft snore. She couldn't wake him. She wouldn't make it through a good-bye. She'd cry and probably tell him everything. She couldn't risk the truth. It would be the only secret she would ever keep from her husband. She prayed he'd be strong enough to make love when she got back home.

Please be better so I can pretend this possible miracle is ours. One time is all I need. Please be well enough to make love like we used to. Before the diagnosis came and everything changed.

Quietly and carefully, Lainie removed herself from the sleeping man. She tiptoed around the room, searching for clothes. She couldn't remember where she took them off. She found his on the floor near the bed, but hers were absent from the area.

She spied her luggage bag near the bathroom. *Did I bring my luggage in here?*

She picked it up trying not to make a sound. She was afraid of waking the man. *No, it's Luke, not just any man. If I have a boy, I'll name him after his father.*

She made it to the front door and found her purse, shoes, and dress folded on top of a cabinet. She opened her bag. With every slight noise she or he made, she became more nervous and perspired. She couldn't get caught. She didn't want to have to explain anything, and his personality would definitely demand an explanation.

She pulled out jeans, bra, and a T-shirt from the bag. She wasn't going to chance opening up her socks and underwear bag. No way. She could go commando to the airport.

She stuffed her dress in the bag and then pulled on her jeans as she glanced down, spying the sparkles from the diamond nipple rings. *Dang. When did I do that?*

She sent up a prayer she wouldn't get stopped by airport security and miss her flight home. She tucked her bra in her suitcase. Pulling the T-shirt over her head and chest, she grazed over her breasts and was surprised that her nipples didn't hurt. Nothing hurt. Her skin even shimmered as if she'd gotten dusted all over with silver glitter.

Weird. Is it from the new lotion sample I put on? The lady didn't mention anything about glitter.

She opened her purse and pulled out her phone. *Crap.* The earliest flight home left in less than two hours. She had to get the hell out of there.

She carried her heels along with her suitcase, bag, and purse, and tiptoed out the door, praying Luke wouldn't wake up until she vanished from Vegas.

Once outside, she hurried to the lobby to check out of her room. She had no idea when she had brought her bag into his room last night, but she chalked it up to being drunk, stupid, or something she couldn't explain.

Henrietta stood fresh and lovely, smiling as if she knew Lainie had slept with Luke.

Lainie bit her bottom lip, ran her fingers through her tangled hair, and walked straight to her friend.

"I need to check out," Lainie said. "Can you call and cancel that class?"

"You're not going to stay?" Henrietta raised her eyebrows and tilted her head to the side.

Lainie rubbed the tender skin over her neck from his love bites. Her belly warmed, and every inch of her body wanted to march right back into that room and go for another round or ten with him.

"No, I need to get back home. How much do I owe you?"

"Nothing," Henrietta said. "You paid cash. You're good. When are you coming back?"

"Um, not sure," Lainie said.

She didn't want to lie and say she'd be back. She had no plans of ever returning, if she was pregnant. And there was a good chance a baby was growing inside her right now.

Regardless of the outcome, she wasn't going to try again. Luke was her one and only shot at having a baby. Cheating on her husband wasn't a habitual thing. Once. Never again.

"Well, when you do, stay with us," Henrietta said.

Lainie smiled. "Of course I will."

"Do you need a cab or shuttle?" Henrietta asked.

"No, ma'am," Lainie replied. "I've got it covered. Thanks for everything."

She turned around, practically ran out of the lobby, and headed for the main strip to hail a taxi to the airport. The only clues she left were her first name and hometown. Everything else was paid by cash. No trails to follow her, not that he would.

Glad she was rushed to catch a flight, she couldn't dwell on abandoning Luke without even a note.

She made it to the airport in record time and got on an early flight to Atlanta. She settled in her first-class seat and exhaled.

"Late night?" the man next to her asked.

"No, sir," Lainie said. "Five o'clock comes too

early for me."

The flight attendants followed along with the safety procedure video as the plane taxied for take-off.

Lainie gazed down as she buckled her seat belt. Her wrists and arms sparkled brightly like they had in the hotel. She rubbed her arms, but the strange silvery sparkles continued to shine.

I'm going to call the lady from the class about that lotion sample. She never mentioned it had special glitter in it.

The flight attendants checked the cabin and then sat in their seats. The plane's engine revved.

The man leaned in and sniffed. It was subtle but obvious enough for her to notice.

"Sorry. I ran down a taxi, and I hope I don't smell bad." She half cringed and half smiled. "I'm really not a morning person."

The plane sped down the runway and gently lifted off the ground. They ascended skyward.

"Going on a business trip?" he asked.

"No, heading home." Lainie gazed out the window at the world below her. The lights of Vegas in the distance. Her chest constricted as if a snake wrapped around her, squeezing her lungs and suffocating her.

She turned to him. Her breaths came in swift, painful tidal waves, dragging all the air out of her lungs with each passing second.

"I'm Lainie. What's your name?" Her voice was barely audible as she tried to act normal.

The man looked at her with the same seemingly curious gaze as Henrietta had.

"I'm Michael Flanagan. I'm originally from

Vegas, but I'm going home to Atlanta. I travel a lot between the two cities for business. Are you okay?"

She nodded. The plane seemed like it was spinning out of control. She reached for the man to steady the spinning, to catch her breath, and to gain composure.

"Head between your knees." He pushed her head down. "Breathe. First time away is hard. Almost impossible to do."

Her heart pounded out of her chest. *I'm going to die. I can't die. Frank needs me. I have to go home.*

"Breathe in," he whispered. "Let the blood get back to your head."

She gasped for air. *I'm not going to make it.*

His warm hand stroked up and down her back, soothing her, relaxing the layers of constricted muscles, allowing air to return to her lungs.

"It's not good to be apart from the one you love."

She nodded.

"I'm okay. I'm okay." She pushed her back against his hand.

He guided her up little by little until her back hit the soft leather seat. "Better?"

"Yes. Thank you."

"No problem. It happens… Not to me." He winked at her.

She would have laughed, but her head wasn't quite back to normal. Instead, she smiled.

"Do you live inside the city?" she asked.

"No, suburbs. Buckhead." Michael shifted in his seat, turning toward her. "What do you do?"

"I work for myself," Lainie said. "What do you do?"

Michael adjusted his blue-and-white-striped tie

and talked her ear off for most of the trip about his financial consulting firm. He fished for more information about her and her business. But, his questions weren't too specific, so she gave general answers. He seemed to want her to be open about her life and career, but she'd learned a long time ago people got weird when she mentioned she was a massage therapist. There would be an awkward joke, a body part shoved at her, or full disclosure of some physical problem from the person.

She wasn't looking for business. She needed a friend, not a client. Luckily, he didn't pry or come close to guessing her real job, so she never really gave him what he wanted. They chatted about the local restaurants and the best places to dine. Her favorite places.

She made a point to keep her answers vague. But she liked him and got closer and closer to telling him a little more about her personal life, something she rarely considered doing with anyone, let alone a stranger.

Michael, on the other hand, told her where he grew up in Vegas, when he moved to Atlanta for business, restaurants he recommended in both cities, and even asked her to join him for dinner the following evening as they exited the plane.

Using work as an excuse, she declined. Making social plans didn't work out often with her husband's illness. If he had a good day, she wanted to celebrate with only him. If he was struggling, she wanted to be there to take care of him.

Together they walked to baggage claim, picked up their luggage, and continued to the parking lot.

She reached out and shook his hand. The shimmering effect on her skin intensified upon contact. Something was definitely up with the lotions and oils she'd sampled all week. She'd get to the bottom of it once she unpacked.

"It was nice meeting you, Michael. I hope you enjoy living in the best state in the Union. Before you know it, you'll be telling everyone you were born and raised here, and never mention that *other* place again."

Michel shook her hand, and chuckled. "Lainie, what's your last name?"

She blushed and shook her head.

"It's Ivanovski. Lainie Ivanovski. I'm sorry. My mother is turning over in her grave at my lack of manners. And thank you for helping with that little panic attack on the plane. I don't know what came over me. I'm usually the most relaxed person in the room."

Michael handed her his business card.

"If your work gets finished and you're in my part of town around eight, call me for dinner. My treat. You can bring your husband."

"Thanks, but I don't expect to be done until ten," Lainie said. "That's too late for my husband and most people."

"Not me," Michael said. "I'm still coming off Pacific Daylight Time. That's my dinnertime."

Lainie laughed, tucking his card into the front pocket of her jeans. "You're right. I'll call you if I can."

"Great," Michael said. "Meet you at ten fifteen at Jules Steakhouse."

"You're funny," Lainie said. "Don't count on me."

"I will, but if you don't show, at least I'll eat well."

"See you later," Lainie said. *I won't be there.*

"Great. Bring your husband. I'd love to meet him."

"We'll see." She walked off to the shuttle for long-term parking.

"Wait up," Michael called after her.

She glanced over her shoulder. Michael hustled toward her. He moved surprisingly smoothly over the sidewalk in his navy designer suit and leather shoes.

"I've got a car waiting." He grabbed her luggage bag near her feet and walked to a black limo.

In any other circumstance, she would have backed away from him, but her gut pushed her feet forward automatically. He seemed concerned for her safety and her well-being, like a man worried about his sister or a close friend.

He placed their luggage next to the trunk. "I'll take you to your car. No reason to wait."

The chauffer held open the back door for them.

"Thanks," she said. "Sometimes the shuttle takes a little longer when Percy is working. He is known to drive around the lot for people who can't remember where they parked as they click their alarm button and listen for it."

"You know the shuttle drivers? Do you travel a lot?"

"Yeah, I do. Percy's a sweet man, but gosh, he can take a while. I know he's working today."

Michael's eyes lit up. "So, do you travel to the same cities for business?"

"Yes, sir," Lainie said. "Mostly Chicago and Manhattan, but occasionally I head out to Los Angeles and San Francisco. I try to limit those trips. I'm really a homebody."

"What exactly do you do?" Michael asked.

The driver glanced back at her through the open window in the center of the front seat rest, seemingly listening as he drove to long-term parking.

Lainie sighed.

"I'm a massage therapist. I know. I know. I don't look like one. I don't act like one. I'm not all tree hugging and new age. I'm a normal, everyday kind of girl. I'm just gifted at what I do."

"And your husband is okay with it?" His head jerked back, knocking the headrest of his seat with a strong thud. "That doesn't seem possible."

"My husband doesn't mind. He knows business is business, and I'm professional. There's the occasional come-on, but it's rare. Everyone I work with knows the deal. If they say or act improperly, they pay me for the infraction, and they are blacklisted from my services. Period. If they refer someone who acts or says something improper, not only is that person banned from my services, but they are too."

"Really? That sounds like a dangerous profession."

She shrugged. "Surprisingly, it can be. But my policies keep me from having to deal with assholes. I travel to clients' homes. Sometimes, I go on a client's business trips or tours. I'm heading to Chicago next week for a couple days for a client."

She looked out the window at the beautiful blue midmorning sky with the sun beating down to scorch everyone. The shuttle bus idled in the middle of an aisle. The gray-haired shuttle driver, Percy, wiped his dirty hands on the hand towel he always kept hanging out his back pocket. He picked up the extra car jack from the side of the sedan and walked toward the bus.

"There's Percy helping that old lady with her flat tire. He's a great guy. Slow down for a second."

The car slowed to a crawl.

She pushed the button to open the window. She stuck her head out.

"Hey, Percy." She waved. "I'll see you later this week."

"Hey there, Miss Lainie." He waved back. "Missed you yesterday. Thought your plane was running late. Then, I remembered you were coming in today. You're early."

"Yes, sir," Lainie said. "I got an earlier flight."

"Be careful driving home. I-20 into the city is backed up something fierce this morning. Tractor trailer tumped over and has four lanes blocked."

"Thanks for the heads-up," Lainie yelled. "Give my best to Trudy, and tell her I loved the peach cobbler. I ate it in the terminal. All of it. I'll probably see you Wednesday."

"Yes, ma'am, Miss. Lainie," Percy said. "E-mail me your schedule once it's confirmed. I'll have Trudy make you some more."

Lainie waved good-bye and rolled up the window. "My car is two rows down on the left."

The driver repeated her instructions and drove right toward it.

"There it is." She pointed to her sports car.

The driver seemed confused as he looked at where she pointed but didn't slow down to let her out.

"Hey, you passed it." She pointed at the back

window. "The Mercedes convertible."

"Your husband fits in that?" Michael asked, raising his brow.

"It's small, but Frank loves it. He's…" She closed her mouth, cutting off the flow of information on the tip of her tongue. She swallowed and started over. "Yeah, he does."

The limo stopped behind her car.

"Frank Ivanovski?" Michael asked. "The music producer?"

She nodded. A lump of emotions clogged her throat. She swallowed hard, clearing the constriction enough to speak.

"Yeah, most people don't recognize the name if they aren't in the biz."

The driver got out of the car and walked around to her side.

"I've heard of him but don't know him," Michael said.

The car door opened. The bright rays of Georgia sunshine highlighted the silver sparkles on her flesh.

"Bring him to dinner," Michael said, sliding closer to her as she adjusted in her seat to leave. "I'm not a musician. I don't have any musicians in my family. I don't consult with any musicians. We won't talk shop since I can't sing worth a damn. We'll talk about something else. How about the great state of Georgia?"

She chuckled internally. "We'll see, Michael Flanagan. I'm going to Google you first to see what kind of serial killer you are."

She stepped out of the limo and dug into her pocket for her keys. A new wave of anxiety flowed through her as she picked up her luggage from the driver. Her fingers clasped tightly around the metal keys.

I don't know why, but I like you. I don't want to leave, but I want to go home.

"Yeah, I'm a consultant who lures hot married women and their husbands to dinner just to bore them to death."

"You sure know how to sweet talk a girl," she laughed. "Fine. Jules Steakhouse at ten fifteen tonight. The reservation will be under Lainie."

"See you then," he said. "Thanks. I really hate eating alone."

"There will be no alone if you and Frank get along."

Hopefully Frank will be up for having dinner out. Maybe the new medicines are working.

"He's going to love me."

"Love might be a tall order, but I do think he'll like you." She lowered her eyes to the concrete below her feet. "At least I hope so."

She opened her door, breathing the scent of new leather and her husband—whiskey and smoke. She tossed her bags into the passenger's side and pivoted, facing Michael.

"Michael, please don't tell anyone about meeting me and Frank," she said. "If there are paparazzi, we're not going into the restaurant. Frank is really private, and so am I. We don't go out much. We really don't leave the house, except for business. When you meet Frank, you'll understand."

You'll see how sick he is. But he'll be better. He's going to get a miracle.

"I wouldn't tell anyone," Michael said. "I'm a

finance guy. Talk about being private. It's why I'm begging a woman I just met to meet me for dinner with her husband. And if she were to bring along a beautiful friend, which would be a bonus." He shook his head. "I'm kidding about the friend. Please don't bring me a date. I've had one too many blind dates lately."

"It will just be me and my husband. See you later." She sank down into the plush driver's seat and shut the door, cutting off the possibility of conversation. She placed the key in the ignition and turned it.

The engine rumbled like the growls that came from…*Luke.*

Her chest constricted inward like a vise crushing her heart. She leaned forward. Her head fell gently against the steering wheel.

Inhale peace. Exhale anxiety. I'm not having a heart attack. It's guilt. It's only guilt. But Frank will be so happy when I tell him we're having a baby. Please let me be pregnant. It will give him even more reason to fight his illness until there's a cure. I can't get in touch with Luke anyway. I only have a first name. It was one night of… God, I was so drunk. Too drunk to even remember it all. I'm never drinking again.

She drew in a deep breath, releasing the heavy pressure fighting to take over.

I can do this.

She sat back and looked around the lot. Michael's car idled nearby. *He's probably making sure I'm okay. Nice man. Big and nerdy, yet calm and comforting.* She needed a friend like him right now. Someone who could be the peaceful influence she usually was for everyone around her.

CHAPTER SIX

S HE PUT THE CAR IN gear and drove out of the parking lot toward home, keeping track of Michael's limo following behind her. Not that it was weird his car was behind hers. They were heading in the same direction. She moved into the right lane, escaping the hectic airport. She glanced into the rearview mirror for Michael's vehicle. His limo switched lanes too. But once she exited onto the interstate, she lost him in a sea of cars.

She phoned Frank.

"Lainie?" Frank rasped. "Good Lord, it's early."

"It's eleven, honey. I'll be home soon. How are you feeling?"

"Like shit but more like a softer shit." He muffled a cough, but she heard it like he was sitting right next to her. "No, baby. I'm doing better than when you left. It's been a tough week at work, and my insides feel like they've been torn out, scrambled in a skillet, and shoved back in."

He stifled another cough. "I've missed you."

"I missed you too. I can't wait to see you." Her voice rose in tone. "I love you." *I love you. I need you. Only you.*

"Did you do anything I need to know about?"

She pressed her lips together to keep from blurting the entire truth out to him. *I have a secret I can't tell you.*

"I kind of did something impulsive. You know sometimes when I go to these massage classes I get wrangled into doing stuff."

He sighed.

She imagined his epic eye roll—the one he used when he was irritated and curious.

"What did you do this time?" he asked.

"Got my nipples pierced." She held her breath, waiting for him to say anything.

He cleared his throat but stayed silent.

"Are you mad? They're kind of sexy with diamonds and stuff. I panicked going through airport security, but it was fine. I didn't get stopped or searched. Next time, I'm flying in your corporate jet."

"You'd still have to clear security." He inhaled. "Do they hurt?"

"Not at all." She hadn't expected him to be so quiet. "Are you mad?" *Does he know about Luke? Did someone you know see me at the hotel?*

"Not mad. I've always had a thing for your tits, and now it seems you've been able to make them sparkle like your personality."

She laughed and then lowered her voice. "First thing I'm doing when I get in is taking a shower. The next thing I'm doing is showing off my piercings to my sexy husband."

"I can't wait."

"There's one more thing," Lainie said. "We're

having dinner at Jules's restaurant at ten tonight with a new friend of mine, Michael Flanagan. He's funny and nice. Are you up for a late dinner?"

"A late dinner sounds good." He coughed, and his chest rattled.

"That doesn't sound good. Are you okay?"

"Yeah," he said. "Just a little cough. The new medicine is helping a lot."

Liar. I guess we're both keeping secrets.

She gripped the steering wheel as she turned off the interstate onto the private road Frank bought and built just for her to get from the house to the airport quickly. The private road was ridiculously excessive, and they'd fought over the construction of it. He had supposedly backed down and quit pursuing the endeavor. She had calmed down, thinking she'd won.

Then, two weeks ago, he drove her to the airport on their new road in the new luxury convertible he bought her. She had complained about the road until it saved her from sitting in traffic because of a pileup on the interstate. He always thought of her first.

She tapped the code on the remote in her car to open the security gate. "Almost there. I'm on our road."

She glanced over at the exit and saw Michael's limo pulling off onto her exit. She drove through the open gate and waved at them as the gate closed behind her.

"As soon as I'm done in the studio, you can come up," he said, his voice a little stronger, sounding more like himself. "I promise I won't be long."

"I'll come and get you if you take too long." She

needed to get back into her routine. *Forget about Vegas. Work on finding a cure. Pray there's a baby growing in my belly. Pray Frank is well enough to have sex. Pray for the miracle to happen today.*

"Baby, sneak into the studio if I'm not out before you leave again," he said. "I really do miss you. But I'm on a deadline. And I'm working with some really good talent."

"I know." *Work keeps you going. Gets you out of bed in the morning.* "You're the best in the business."

"Just like you, baby."

Phone static and hard hacking coughs filled her ears.

"Got to go so I can finish up and give you the homecoming you deserve," he rasped and ended the phone call.

You have to get better. And I've got to get home and wash off the evidence of last night.

CHAPTER SEVEN

CURTIS JOHNSON, THEIR HOUSEHOLD MANAGER, stood holding the door open to her Roman-architecture-inspired home. His normally curly gray hair was slicked back straight, and his usually pale skin held a little red tint from being out in the sun too long. He looked more like an Italian mobster from the 1950s than a sixty-six-year-old country boy from Georgia. The dark suit and tie added another level of authenticity to his new look.

"You're looking dapper." *Kind of.* She clenched her jaw as she broke out in a smile. *Not the best look for you.*

He rolled his brown eyes as a light pink flush filled his tanned cheeks. "It was the grandbabies' idea, Miss Lainie, not mine."

She stepped over the threshold into the bright open foyer. "I think you look, um, great. But, I like you in regular jeans and T-shirts a little more. Are you going out tonight?"

"No, ma'am. I've got the four grandbabies coming over to play. I'm supposed to be a famous

British spy." He closed the door and guided her farther into her home. "Your bath is ready for you."

"Thank you, sir." She glanced around the house as she walked down the hallway, passing room after room. Frank had changed something, but she couldn't put her finger on what it was.

"What has he done now?"

Curtis made a strangled throat noise and glanced away from her. "Are you talking about the freshly painted walls?"

"Spill the rest."

"He made some renovations. The bedroom is larger, and there's all new furniture. But don't yell at him. Not today."

The worry in Curtis's voice seemed to beat at her chest, mimicking her own fears that Frank wasn't strong enough to handle any confrontation.

"How bad is he? Should I cancel my trip to Chicago?"

"Maybe take the next couple months off." His steps faltered the closer they moved toward her bedroom.

He stopped, took in a deep breath, and moved forward at a snail's pace, as if he carried too heavy a load on his shoulders.

Moisture filled her eyes. "Could you tell Marla to clear my schedule for the next six months? I made dinner plans for tonight. Should I cancel those?"

"No. He's having a good day. He'd be mad if he heard me talking to you about…" He glanced at the bedroom door ahead and back at her. "You're already confirmed to go to your afternoon and evening appointments. Mr. Frank will be in the studio for the rest of the evening."

She glanced into the open bedrooms as they progressed toward the master suite. He'd redecorated all the rooms in the areas she'd passed.

"What got into him?"

Curtis took her hand and curled her arm around his. They walked arm in arm, supporting each other.

"I almost called you to come home Wednesday when he couldn't keep anything down. He put up such a fuss that I didn't. Furniture delivery guys, painters, and decorators swarmed the house, making changes all week. Then I really was ready to call you when he stayed in bed all day Thursday. But when nightfall came, he ate a full meal and looked good. His Friday appointment went well. He came home and worked all day and into the evening. He's been in the studio since you called. Energized and happy."

She nodded. *You're lying for him. Something serious happened. Please just tell me.*

He guided her into the master suite.

The heavy scent of disinfectant smacked her in the face, nearly knocking her down. She stumbled, but Curtis must have known it was coming, because his hold was stronger than usual. Frank had to have been hospital sick while she was gone.

"Tell Marla I'm taking a sabbatical. Tell her to cancel everything on my calendar for the year. Tell her to make something up about some new technique I'm submerging myself in. And make an appointment with Frank's oncologist."

"He's already seen him." He glanced away from her. "We all missed you, but Mr. Frank missed you most of all."

She wrapped her arms around him, clinging to the only other person she trusted to have Frank's best interest at heart. "You should have called. Was he in the hospital? Did you at least call a nurse?"

He nodded.

"The doctor was here. We took him to the hospital," he whispered as he kissed the top of her head. "There, there. He got through it. He's a strong man. You needed a break."

"No. I n-need—" She tried to control her voice from breaking but failed, feeling as fragile as a piece of glass millimeters from shattering on the ground. "Frank is all I need. I never should have left."

"No. A baby would give him another reason to keep going."

She stiffened in his embrace.

"It'll be okay," Curtis whispered. "I'll never say a word if you end up pregnant. I know y'all have been praying for one for a long time." He patted her on her back like he was comforting one of his grandchildren. "Don't you worry. We all know how much you love him. A week in another man's arms is understandable after the past year."

"I didn't—"

"Darlin', what I'm saying is, it doesn't matter what you did. We know your heart, and we know his. There isn't anything either of you wouldn't do for the other. And, we know you deserve some comforting too."

She nodded as moisture dotted her eyes. She swallowed over and over, trying to stop the flood of emotions threatening to overwhelm her and sending her into the empty place she lived before Frank came into her life. She wouldn't survive without him. She needed a miracle.

He held her, but the comfort she wished for wasn't something he could give her.

"I need him to live." Her lungs revolted against her chest rising in thin layers as she tried to breathe. "I…love…him."

"I know. We all know." He straightened up and squared his shoulders like he had every time he was done hugging her over the years. "You've got to be strong. Go take a bath, and get yourself smelling all nice like you do. Then, go see that stubborn man in his studio."

"He's not going to make it another month is he?"

His hands slid down her arms and let go of her at her wrists. Fluid filled his eyes as he turned from her. He shook his head.

"We're glad you're home."

He walked out of her bedroom and closed the door behind him.

She sank to the floor as the fantasy of them together—a happy family with a baby on the way—was crushed.

CHAPTER EIGHT

IN THE LATE AFTERNOON, LUKE woke up in an empty bed. He stretched his tired arms and sore legs.

Where is my beautiful mate?

"Lainie?"

She couldn't have gone far. Maybe she went to get us something to eat.

He smiled. Yep. She was already taking care of him, looking after his needs, not just her own.

He inhaled deeply, searching for his mate's scent. He didn't catch it anywhere near him. He didn't want to entertain the possibility she left without telling him where she planned to go. She was human, but she wouldn't take off without him. She couldn't leave. Not after last night. Not to him. Mates don't leave. Ever.

His heart ricocheted off his chest.

"Fuck."

He hopped off the bed and groaned. *Damn, I'm not recovered. Is she?*

He ignored the pangs in his body and the ache in his chest and threw on jeans and a T-shirt.

His wolf pushed against the surface of his skin. There were no other scents in the room. No other pack came in and took her while he was passed out.

She left me. No. She couldn't have. I'm the Alpha. We bonded. We mated. Someone took her for leverage. I'm going to find him and kill him.

He grabbed his keycard and hauled ass to the lobby.

He walked up to the counter.

"Mr. Wolfson," Kelly, the day concierge, said. "How may I help you?"

"Where's Henrietta?"

"She'll be in at seven. Is there anything I can help you with?"

Luke opened his mouth and then shut it.

"Sir?"

"Henrietta's number."

Kelly hesitated. "Um." She typed into her computer. "Is she in trouble?"

"No."

Kelly quickly jotted down Henrietta's cell on a blue sticky note.

Luke nodded. "I'll see you next month at the pack meeting."

"Yes, sir, Alpha, sir." Kelly lowered her gaze.

Luke jogged back to his room and dialed Henrietta.

"Hello?" Henrietta yawned loudly. "Sorry. Hello?"

"Hey, it's Luke Wolfson."

"Is something wrong at the hotel?" Henrietta asked.

"No, I met…" *My mate.* "I met a woman named

Lainie last night."

"Yeah," Henrietta said. "She left this morning around four to go home. Hasn't she returned yet? Mates don't go far."

"Where is she from? Do you have a last name?"

"Don't know much about her. She paid cash for the room and advanced incidentals on arrival. She was taking a massage therapy class. She only went by her first name. She was from somewhere down South. Birmingham? Atlanta? Memphis? I can't remember. She couldn't have boarded the plane. She's probably on the strip eating. Mating consumes an incredible amount of calories."

"You don't know her last name?" *What? That is impossible.*

"She stayed with us because we're lax on stuff like that. She works with celebrities and keeps a low profile. Wait. She's a massage therapist from Atlanta."

"Do you have a phone number?" Luke asked.

"Yes, but it was disconnected. Sorry, Alpha. I told her I'd add her name to another class she was going to take, only the instructor had never heard of her." She yawned again. "She's not going to leave town. She's probably confused and hungry."

He covered his cell with his hand, ready to scream. He brought it back up to his face. "Just found her note under the bed. I'm going to get her."

"Great. She seemed a little freaked out this morning. She's not a one-night-stand kind of girl. Humans are just different about sex, but you know that. Glad you found her note."

He was about to hit the End button when he remembered the negative feedback he'd gotten about his abrupt hang-ups at the latest Alpha-only International Pack Conference.

Damn sensitivity training.

"Sorry for interrupting your sleep. See you at the meeting."

"Aww. Thank you, Alpha."

He rolled his eyes as he tapped the screen, ending the call. *It's the little things with the girls.*

He texted Danny to meet for an emergency meeting. He had to find her before she morphed into a wolf. He had to find her before some stray werewolf or… *Grrrrrr.*

If she'd left his territory. If she was in the Southeast wandering around unprotected with his scent all over her… *No. No. No. No. If she dies, I die. Our baby… No.*

He tore the sheets from the bed and gathered them up. His chest tightened. His heart stopped. Darkness came over him. *No. You're not coming out. You're not…*

He fell to his hands and knees. His gums tingled. *We'll find her,* the wolf inside him said.

His ears and nose burned as they stretched. His beast pushed to take control. It would be so easy to let him come out. But if she was gone, he needed a clear head. He needed… *I'll call in help. We'll find her.*

Droplets of sweat ran down his forehead to his nose and splattered on the wooden floor.

She's not here. She left us. You let her leave us. I'm going to find her. I'm going to get her. Let. Me. Out, the wolf demanded.

His hands squeezed into tight fists, halting the beast. *I need to travel possibly a long distance to get her.*

His beast receded from forcing the change, allowing him to breathe again.

Fuck. I'm going to have to call Michael.

CHAPTER NINE

THE CAB DROPPED LUKE OFF at his secured home on the exclusive golf course he designed, built, and owned. Bold yellow-and-orange marigolds blooming in clay pots of varying sizes sat on the smooth concrete porch. His lone juniper tree seemed to straighten from its crooked spine and stretch up toward the sun.

He typed in the security code to the right of the front double doors.

He sniffed. *Danny.*

He opened the door to the right and strode forward onto the handmade Italian tiled floor, frowning. *I should be carrying my mate over the threshold. I should be ripping off her clothes and making love to her right now on this beautiful floor.*

"Where's Lainie?" Danny asked, standing up from the cushioned bench in front of the entrance to the sitting room.

"I have no fucking idea, or I'd be with her. Henrietta said she thinks she's from the South but not our South." His hands tingled to shift, to fight, and to find her. "She thinks Lainie is from Michael's territory. Specifically, Atlanta, Georgia."

With Danny by his side, he strode past the formal sitting room, formal dining room, the gathering room, and into his office.

"Are you going to call Michael?" Danny's cheek twitched.

His wolf itched to surface.

Luke's beast growled.

Simmer down. We'll find her.

"You said the meeting with Michael wasn't horrible," Danny said.

"I hope she's not in Atlanta," Luke said.

"I'll call and tell him I goofed up," Danny offered. "I'll ask him for help privately."

Luke sat down at his desk.

"Not yet. Let's get in touch with the Alphas of our pack first. If she isn't located in my territory within a few hours, I'll call him." His shoulders slumped. He and Danny had been friends since birth. "This really sucks, man."

Danny gripped Luke's shoulder. "I'm sorry. She must have had a good reason for leaving."

"Yeah, that's what I'm afraid of," Luke said. "I don't know a damned thing about her, and now she's vanished. I can't believe she paid cash for everything. Who does that anymore?"

"You do," Danny said.

"Yeah, but I'm not like most people," Luke said.

"Yeah, you're rich," Danny said. "The rest of us peasants use credit cards."

"She's a massage therapist," Luke said, powering up his computer. "That usually doesn't make you rich."

"I don't know. Maybe she's independently

wealthy or something," Danny said. "Her dress was really nice, and her shoes looked designer."

Luke shook his head.

"The dress was a knockoff, and the shoes were designer three years ago. I shouldn't know that. But during the presentation from the female Alpha of France at the conference this week, we were all forced to watch slides of the latest designer outfits."

"Sure, man," Danny teased him. "You were *forced* to pay attention."

Luke let out a halfhearted laugh.

"Everyone was staring at me. I know they expected me to walk out." He logged on and checked his e-mail. "At least Michael hasn't called. If he found her, I'd never hear the end of it."

"How long before you think she'll shift into a wolf?" Danny asked.

"I need to find her before the next full moon."

"I'll contact our detectives," Danny said with his thumbs tapping on his phone. "I'll also check on those vacationing in Michael's territory and see if they've heard about or scented her."

"It's got to stay private. Only contact our detectives. If this got out…" His heart pounded with adrenaline to get moving, to run, and to find her. *Need her with me. Need her safe.*

Danny nodded.

"It's not getting out. No one will go up against you. You're getting sworn in as Alpha over the American continents at the next full moon." Danny sucked in, attempting to hide his gasp. "Shit. She's got to be there."

"Yes. She *will* be there." Luke stared at the computer screen showing a list of flights from Vegas to Atlanta. He hadn't remembered typing on the keyboard or searching for flights. *She's there. Not Birmingham, Miami, or Memphis. Peaches. My succulent Atlanta, Georgia, peach.*

"She left town. Jack checked her through security at the airport. Nonstop flight to Atlanta, Georgia." Danny said. "Under a different name. Elaine something that started with an 'I' or a 'V.'"

"Thanks. Take care of things here. I'm going alone." Luke booked the next flight out and started searching for her on the Internet. He'd have to call Michael. There was no way around it.

"I can call Michael's brother, Gabriel. Get him involved on our side."

"No. The Flanagans are a pain in the ass. Damn it. Why did she have to fly there? The fucking Georgia Pack. Michael's their personal Alpha." He growled. His pulse raced as his skin began to tingle and itch.

His fingers flew over the keyboard. Google. Nothing. Massage. Nothing. Elaine I and V. Lainie. Nothing. His mate had vanished into thin air.

"She's a fucking ghost." He bolted up from his chair. His hands slammed down on his desk. His eyes drifted in and out of focus as his beast pushed for control.

"The Flanagans aren't that bad," Danny said. "They'll help. They'd call you if something like this happened to one of them."

"I know. It's just that it's me and him. If my mate lives in the southeast"—his stomach knotted—"then she's part of *his* pack. I have to— *grrrr*—ask him permission to marry her."

"Call him as a friend," Danny said. "You two

used to be good friends before the regions got divvied up."

Grrrr.

Danny raised his hands in surrender, backing out of the room.

"Fine. It's your decision, but I think you should c-call…only." He cleared his throat. "If you want to…uh… Maybe, if you feel like…You're growling like you're going to… Shit. I'll find her last name and text you." Danny turned and ran out of the room.

Closing his eyes, Luke imagined her lovely blue gaze staring into his. The call to track her down consumed him. His power as Alpha compelled him to find the growing beast inside his mate. He had to retrieve her before Michael got involved. He had to link to her mind, body, soul, and wolf.

Envisioning a thick-braided rope extending from his heart, he called to the Alphas of his territory, strengthening the special connection of their packs to find the one wolf missing. One by one they joined until they reached Michael Flanagan's territory.

With only a few weeks until he was Continent Alpha over Michael's region, he rationalized circumventing Michael's involvement. Michael would be under his authority soon.

Luke used his Alpha ability and followed the unified conscience of the pack to track her. He mentally crossed the border, commanding Michael's wolves to obey him. He formed new pack links and designated his authority over the east side of North America. He took in their experiences. He memorized scents, sightings, and tastes, searching to discover his mate's aroma and her home. The scent of peaches, peanuts, and pine grew stronger until it was her. His mate. His love. His life. His home.

Luke, she sighed, answering his call through her thoughts.

His cock hardened.

Yes, Lainie. It's me. I'm coming.

He expanded his power through their new link as her Alpha and mate. He searched to find the permanent connection to her wolf and to her.

Call me, Michael Flanagan interrupted, abruptly severing the connection with his mate and unraveling the link to the wolves in Michael's jurisdiction.

She was gone.

He opened his eyes and took a deep breath in.

Michael found her first. I'm fucked.

CHAPTER TEN

LAINIE PACKED UP HER SHEETS and oils into separate bags near the exit to the hallway instead of the bedroom her client liked to show off. Her policy of staying out of bedrooms was usually enough, but this particular client insisted the massage take place in the spacious spalike bathroom. Beautiful imported tile from Greece, elegant silk fabric panels hung from the ceilings separating the three-person bathtubs that she knew exactly what the client and her spouse used for.

Don't go there.

Normally, the bathroom was sparkling clean, but when she arrived, sex toys soaked in sudsy water in the dual sinks. The heavy scent of intercourse threw her off her game. Mirrors had been recently installed over the entire ceiling and most of the walls of the room. She couldn't look anywhere without seeing her client and herself. It was overwhelming and dizzying. Maybe she'd open a spa once Frank got better. She was tired of landing in situations like these.

"Next Saturday at two would be fabulous. I'd like

you to massage a dear friend before me too," Ginger said, opening the middle drawer of the vanity cabinet. She pulled out a silver tray and a tube of lubricant. She closed the drawer and opened the top one. She rummaged around, making too much noise for Lainie to answer immediately. Control. The woman always needed to control everything.

"I can't. I'm taking some time off and immersing myself in classes about manual lymphatic drainage." *I'm not going to do another massage in this room. I'm not one of your submissives.*

"But you already do that." Ginger picked up a flat brush and inspected it.

"Yes, but I need the refresher. You'll reap the benefits when I finish my training. But no more massages in this room. Next time…" *If there is a next time.* "You need to set up the table in a room where there is no bedroom access."

Ginger frowned. She carefully placed the brush down on the tray. "I didn't do anything to upset you. Did I?"

"No, no," Lainie reassured her. *Yes. A little. Damn it.*

"I'm not going to ask you to do anything sexual. I understand you have to be careful in your business. It's one of the reasons I like you so much. You follow rules and don't deviate from them."

"I know," she answered. *We went through limits in the first session. I should add "no prepping for your sex partners while I'm still in the room."* "I'm canceling my entire calendar for the rest of the year. Maybe longer. I want to take an extended vacation with my husband too. We haven't had time for a long trip since our honeymoon."

"Oh. Who are you married to again?" She traced her diamond necklace, drawing Lainie's gaze to the sparkles that reminded her of Vegas and...*Luke.*

"I don't think you know him." *I'm sure you know him. He has produced all your husband's music for the past ten years.*

"How can you afford to take a year off work?" The pretty redhead handed Lainie a check for her services.

Ginger always pissed her off with the whole I've-got-more-money-than-God routine.

"Money isn't an issue." *Bitch. And you're off my calendar forever.* "I do this because I love it." *And I'm not loving it right now.*

Lainie's phone vibrated. She pulled it out and looked at the message.

I'm here. Waiting for you. My gorgeous wife. You are late.

"I've got to go. My car is waiting." *I should have driven myself. I do not want Ginger to know anything about me, or she will be doing that Domme thing that gets me talking more than I should.*

"Your car?" Ginger rolled her eyes and laughed. "Since when?"

Bitch. Drop the obnoxious act.

The doorbell rang.

Shit. Please don't be Frank at the door.

She hustled to get her bags. Frank hated waiting. She needed to go, or he would be standing outside the door on the next ring. If she was at one of her normal clients' homes, it wouldn't matter so much, but Ginger... *Ugh.*

Fluffing her beautiful red hair, Ginger haughtily sauntered down the ornate hallway toward the entrance.

Lainie bounced her stuffed bags on her shoulders, adjusting them, and quickly caught up to her client.

Ginger opened the gold plated door. She dropped her "I'm better than you" expression and smiled. "Hey, Frank."

Frank frowned. "Ginger."

He stood stiff as a board as Ginger leaned forward and kissed both his cheeks.

"What a surprise." Ginger's green eyes lit up. "Are you here for *me*?"

"Lainie," Frank said, reaching for and taking Lainie's hand.

Ginger's head snapped back as if someone had just hit her. Her green eyes seemed to widen. Her mouth gaped. She made that half huff, half cough sound in the base of her throat as if it was incomprehensible that Frank would prefer a massage therapist over an old-money Southern belle Domme.

"You were supposed to wait in the car," Lainie whispered, glaring at him. *You're not up for walking this much. I should have canceled dinner.*

Ginger pulled herself together in record time. "How do you know Frank?"

"She's my wife," Frank answered, gently tugging Lainie's hand. "Has been for the last eight years."

Lainie and Frank walked down the short steps to the limo, leaving Ginger at her door.

"I didn't know you worked on Ginger," Frank said.

"You know I can't talk about my clients. The whole legal, government, healthcare, privacy thing."

Frank leaned over and kissed her lips. "Sorry. I'm not a patient man, but I love you."

"I love you too. I'm going to cancel dinner. We'll do it another time." *Others might not notice how skinny and tired you are, but I do.*

He opened the car door.

She slid into the back, set her bag on the floorboard on the opposite side of them, and pulled her phone from her front pocket.

Frank slid in next to her and placed his hand over her phone.

"I am sorry. Had I known it was Ginger, I would have never come out. I didn't know they'd moved. I don't want to go home. I want dinner at a nice restaurant with my beautiful wife."

She exhaled and searched his handsome face for signs of deceit. The makeup he'd put on to hide the dark circles, the gaunt cheeks, and the rash from the medicines he took daily was heavier than ever. His normally vibrant blue eyes seemed duller, even with the twinkle they always showed for her.

"You know I love you?"

"That is precisely why we are going to Jules's and eating like royalty," he said. "I'm excited to meet your friend."

"Is that a knock about me not having friends, Mr. Ivanovski?"

"Sweetheart, you've got to get out more, and I'm not talking work." He turned his head away from her.

"I don't need anyone but you." She placed her hand on his thigh. Something new inside her chest whimpered almost mimicking her weakened hope for a miracle. She squashed the sounds wanting to be released but couldn't silence whatever it was inside her from voicing her sadness.

"You do," he whispered. He shifted in his seat, facing her once more. "But right now, I want to see those pretty breasts."

She turned toward him. She was sad but smiling.

"These?" She lifted her T-shirt up over her chest.

"Take it off. Bra too." He licked his lips. His lids dropped to half-mast, covering most of the blue in his eyes.

"No showing them off to others." She pulled the shirt over her head and dropped it to the floor.

"No way. You're my lady, not my possession."

"I'm your lady and your possession." She slid her tongue over her lips, wetting them and then rubbing them together.

"Bra. Take it off." His breathing accelerated. "God, you're sexy."

It had been so long since he'd felt good enough for sex or play. She unhooked her bra and shimmied for him.

He guided her hand from his thigh to his thick cock. "I want to make love to you right now."

She unzipped her jeans and peeled them off, taking her panties to the floor too.

He removed his blue T-shirt as she unbuttoned his designer jeans. He lifted his hips, and she tugged his jeans down over his…

She bit her bottom lip to keep from crying. His once powerful thighs had withered away.

Fluid pricked at her eyes. That horrible whimper inside her revealing the ache in her heart and in her chest. The truth she wanted to ignore became louder and more persistent.

"Climb on my lap, Lainie. You're so gorgeous. So alive."

She straddled his legs. *Careful. Don't hurt him. He's fragile. So. Fragile.*

Sheer willpower to have the moment with him made her pussy produce enough moisture to keep going.

Closing her eyes, she held his hard cock and lowered inch by inch onto his shaft.

He moaned, dropping his head back against the headrest. "I missed you so much."

She leaned forward, finding the meatiest part of his thin neck, and nuzzled. Chemicals. Smoke. Death. A high-pitched squeak escaped through her closed lips.

"Does it hurt?" He moaned. "I… Oh God, Lainie."

"So good." Her voice and breath hitched. She rose and lowered onto him, gently rocking back and forth and carefully grinding.

"Nothing is better than this." His hands caressed up and down her back. "Promise me, you'll move on when I'm—"

"No. Never." She shook her head. *You're not going to die. You're not leaving me.*

Her heart stopped beating. Her lungs stopped expanding for oxygen. Tears won their battle with her eyes.

"You have to." He cupped her face and lifted her head. "Look at me."

She shook her head. Her throat tried to swallow down the painful words, the miserable thoughts of a life without him, but no amount of swallowing could force down the endless train wreck of emotions she held in.

"Sweetheart, look at me," he begged.

Shaking her head, she opened her watery eyes to his heavy gaze.

"This is the first time in eight years you've made social dinner plans. You're all business and me. I love how much you love me. I love how much you love your work."

"I don't want to do this now. Make love to me." She blinked, trying to stop the tears, but the river waters kept rushing over the banks of the dam and down her face.

His lips pressed to hers as if he was suddenly as desperate as she was to forget their reality. She parted her lips and her teeth, as he did his.

He thrust his hips up and groaned. His tongue slid between her teeth.

She held her breath as smoke and mint slid against her tongue. She'd never smelled or tasted anything like it. She shouldn't be so sensitive. She'd never been before, but she hadn't been this raw in years. He always built her up, loved her, and showed her the kind of life worth living. She'd become successful in business because of the confidence he'd filled her with. Without him, she'd die.

He slid his hands into her long hair and devoured her mouth. His chest rose, rubbing against her breasts.

He thrust and grunted, hitting a sweet spot inside her.

Her pussy rippled.

The feeling she couldn't name inside her whimpered. Her voice squeaked as she moved off his lap and pulled him down over her as her back hit the leather of the seat. She caressed down his back, over his hips.

In one feat of strength, he tore his mouth from hers as he thrust like he used to—like he was strong, powerful, and unstoppable.

"Come, Lainie."

She blew apart as pleasure and sorrow mixed together and formed an indestructible bond.

"Yes," he shouted. Spurts of liquid filled her center as he collapsed on top of her. "I'm sorry. I'm so sorry. I don't want to die. I don't want to die."

He buried his face against her neck. He sniffled as his tears moistened her neck.

"I promised myself." He swallowed. "If I made it through this week, I would make love to you. I would give us this last chance for a baby. For a piece of me to live inside you, to grow, and to remind you how much I loved you."

"Please don't," she begged. "Please, not now."

"The hospice nurse came today. She's moving in right now. This is my last night out."

"No. You're good. We made love. You're going to get better." She could barely catch her breath. "We might be having a baby."

"We're not having a baby. It was a dream. An impossible dream."

"Anything's possible. Anything." Her voice held no strength or conviction.

He sighed, shaking his head. "It's not. The hospice nurse told me the pain meds she gave me will work for a few hours."

He coughed. His entire body shuddered.

"Oh God, Frank. Do you need help?" *Please, don't die.*

He pushed upright, coughing and hacking. He held his hand over his mouth as more rounds of coughing continued.

She grabbed the medical kit below the seat and handed him tissues and wipes. The suffocating scent of smoke and death seemed to surround her.

She ran her hands along his ribs, finding more sunken skin between his bones. *Inoperable. Terminal. Incurable. Fatal.*

Her head hung low as his coughing subsided.

"I'm okay." He grabbed the blue T-shirt from the seat near the door.

He exhaled. He reached under the seat and grabbed a clothing box. He set it on her lap. "I saw this on the Internet and had to buy it for you. Don't be angry."

She opened the white box and uncovered a gorgeous ruby choker, an elegant navy lace cocktail dress, and crimson heeled sandals. "I'm not angry. I'll cherish it all."

"Since you're indulging me." He held out his hand.

She placed her left hand in his.

He slid a beautiful princess-cut diamond ring onto her finger.

"I want everyone to see you're mine tonight. Get dressed. Your friend has got to be wondering where we are."

She dressed, following his order. The strength to argue about his extravagant purchases was gone.

Chapter Eleven

THE CAR DOOR OPENED, AND Frank stepped out of the limo onto the concrete sidewalk. She held his hand as she joined him.

He pulled her closer to him and brushed the wayward tears from under her eyes. "You, my love, need to eat."

Her lips trembled as she smiled. "You do."

"Lainie…" He stopped from saying something and instead smiled. "Okay. Let's go meet your new friend."

Walking toward the black exterior of Jules's Restaurant with white lettering and five simple overhead lights shining on the tinted glass entrance, she held on to him a little tighter, steadied him a little more, and wished for more time.

The new, edgy entry added a mysterious factor to the steakhouse, bringing in not only the music industry leaders who made the place famous but also the fashion house mavens moving into that section of town. The longer, narrow walkway to the entrance seemed to be the waiting room for the paparazzi following celebrities in the area.

Inside the dimly lit entry, the hostess greeted them wearing a black dress instead of her signature red. "Your guest is here. Let me show you to your table."

Lainie spied Michael sitting at a red-and-black linen-covered table staring at her. He stood up immediately and waved.

She nodded, made eye contact, and smiled.

The tall brunette guided them through the center of the restaurant past all the regular musicians packed into the red-and-black-themed dining room.

Frank smiled and exchanged greetings as each group of musicians clamored to be noticed. By the time they made it to their table, Michael had been standing for a while.

Lainie shook Michael's hand.

"Michael Flanagan, this is my husband, Frank Ivanovski. Thanks for meeting us here."

Michael breathed in, seemingly sniffing them.

She muffled a laugh. *What the heck? I shouldn't smell bad. He must have a thing about scents.*

Frank shook Michael's hand. "Mr. Flanagan, call me Frank. I hope you didn't have to wait too long, but it's Lainie's fault. She was too polite to her client."

Michael laughed. "She definitely needs to work on saying no more often. Tonight's dinner is a testament to her politeness."

Lainie shook her head and rolled her eyes. "Whatever."

Frank pulled out her chair, and she sat down on a black-leather parson chair. He and Michael stood, waiting for the other to sit first.

"On the count of three, both of you will sit," she said. "One. Two. Three."

The men sat down opposite each other as if they were in some kind of competition. *Men and their testosterone. Don't compare dicks, please.*

"That was some command," Michael said. "Can you teach me that?"

"Good luck." Frank placed his hand on her thigh under the table. "I've been trying to learn it for years, and I still can't do it."

"Enough Lainie bashing, okay?"

Frank leaned over and kissed her. "No more teasing if you don't yell at me for spending money on you."

Lainie closed her eyes and nodded. All her playfulness disappeared.

"Since when does a woman mind it when a man spends money on her?" Michael asked. "I thought that's what we're supposed to do."

"Not for my Lainie," Frank said. "It's a turnoff, big-time. I almost lost my chance with her on our very first date."

"Don't bore him with that story," she said, her heart aching to go back to those days and live them over and over and over again. "It's embarrassing."

The waitress arrived at the table, interrupting them.

"Mr. Ivanovski, I'm Becky, your waitress for this evening. What would you like to drink?" she asked, smiling and showing off a beautiful set of straight white teeth.

Frank looked at Lainie. "We'll have two of Jules's cranberry iced teas with orange slices along with water. Michael, would you like one?"

"Sure. Thanks," Michael said.

"I'll be right back with your drinks." Becky swiftly disappeared into the crowded dining room.

"Now that she's gone," Michael said. "I want to hear all about your first date."

Lainie groaned as Frank told him about their blind date.

"She had no idea who I was and kept asking me what band I was with." Frank laughed. "I got such a kick out of it until the waiter started serenading me."

"Really? The waiter actually sang to you?" Michael asked. "On your date?"

"Yeah," Frank said. "It happens all the time."

He leaned across the table to Michael as Michael leaned in to hear. "I bet you a hundred bucks the waitress will end up singing for me, unsolicited, before the dinner is over."

"Don't bet him." Lainie reached over and touched his hand, noticing the shimmer she'd thought was gone suddenly appear all over her arms. *What kind of weird lotion is this?*

She quickly took inventory of her bare skin. She positively glowed with silver glitter.

"Did you put something on your skin?" Frank asked. "Did I just miss that shimmering sheen?"

"I think it's from those lotion samples I got at the class this week. One of them had a little glitter in it, but this is ridiculous. I'm going to have to call someone. It comes and goes like a mood ring. It's so weird."

"Have Marla call about it. I like it. You should get more," Frank said.

Michael cleared his throat and raised his right

brow. "I concur. The mark…um. The sparkles complement your lovely skin."

Frank kissed her cheek. "So, do *you* want to bet me about the waitress, sweetheart?"

"Uh." She cocked her head to the side and then back. "Nuh-uh."

"I'll bet you the waitress doesn't," Michael said. "I'm sure she's been warned not to."

"She's definitely been warned, but she'll do it anyway," Frank said. "I bet you another hundred she sucks and can't carry a tune to save her life."

Michael laughed. "What makes you say that?"

"I don't know," Frank said. "It's a hunch."

"You're not setting me up, are you? Do you know her?" Michael lowered his chin and glared at her. "He's not setting me up. Is he?"

She rolled her eyes. "No, he's not. But don't bet against him. You'll lose."

"I'll up the stakes and bet you can carry a tune better than she can," Frank said, grinning from ear to ear.

Michael tapped his fingers on the table. "Maybe I can sing."

"No, you can't," Frank said confidently. "Or you'd already be singing for me."

The waitress arrived with drinks and set them down on the table. Wearing the same big, happy grin as before, she stared at Frank as if he hung the moon and the stars just for her.

"What would you like for dinner, sir?"

Frank matched her enthusiasm. He loved to win.

"I'd like two of the house specials cooked medium, please. Michael, my friend, did you get a chance to look at the menu?"

"I'd like the house special also. Cooked *rare*, please."

"Signature salads?" Becky asked.

"No, thank you," Frank said. "Just the specials."

"Okay, sir." Becky lost a little bit of her animated smile. "If you're interested in our chocolate lava cake with raspberry mousse, I should put in the order now."

"We'll take three," Lainie said.

Becky floated away, seemingly thrilled to put in the order.

"Okay, so you get serenaded by the waiter on your date," Michael said. "What happened next?"

"Lainie told the waiter to find some kind of record producer to serenade." Frank's lips formed a tight smile, and he chuckled. "The waiter looked at her like she was from another planet."

"Not one of my finer moments." She pulled the long blonde and light brown strands of hair against her cheek and behind her ear. "Frank laughed so hard he spilled his glass of water, which got the waiter trying to sing and clean up the mess while the owner of the restaurant quickly walked toward the guy. It was a disaster."

"No, it wasn't," Frank said. "It was the best first date I'd ever been on. I paid for our drinks, and we left without eating. I wanted to impress Lainie, since she didn't quite understand who she was on a date with. So I brought her to a boutique for a new dress. She darn near snapped my head off. I knew I loved her as soon as her face turned fire-engine red in righteous indignation. She yelled and screamed at me about what kind of nerve I had thinking I could buy her. It was the most innocent thing I'd ever done. I just wanted to impress her, and I pissed her off."

"It wasn't that bad." She lowered her gaze, her cheeks burning with embarrassment. *It was worse than that. I hit you. Do you remember that, Frank?*

"The hell it wasn't." Frank cupped her chin, making her meet his gaze that sparkled like stars. "They still talk about the night you punched my arm and walked out of the shop without me. I damn near tackled you down in the middle of the street, so you wouldn't get away."

He turned back to Michael. "I took her to the closest fast-food restaurant, and we ate hamburger value meals. It was the cheapest date I'd ever been on with the most beautiful lady I'd ever seen in my life. I would have proposed to her that night if I thought she would've agreed."

"Michael doesn't want to hear about us. You're making me sound silly and naive and…awful."

"No way, baby." Frank slid his arm around her shoulders. "You haven't changed a bit since the first day we met. You're beautiful. Feisty. *Perfect.*"

"So how long have you been married?" Michael asked.

"Eight years," Frank said. "The best eight years of my life."

"Do you have kids?" Michael asked.

"No," Frank said. "What about you?"

Michael took a sip of his drink and opened his mouth to answer when a woman started singing painfully off pitch.

They all gazed toward the awful sound as Becky strutted like a model on a runway toward their table, singing an unrecognizable song for Frank.

Michael pulled out his wallet. He slid two crisp hundred-dollar bills across the table to Frank as Becky finished her little audition.

Lainie clapped for her.

"Sorry, Becky." Frank pocketed Michael's money. "I'm not the producer for you."

"But I can sing you something else." The waitress smiled. "Please?"

"No, darling," Frank said, dashing her dreams from being discovered by him. "Maybe some other time, but we're in a business meeting and need some privacy."

"Oh, sorry." Becky slid a CD across the table to Frank.

Frank ignored the gesture, but Lainie took the CD and slipped it into her purse.

Becky looked at her with hope in her amber eyes and left them alone.

"I told you not to bet against him," she said.

"It was only two hundred dollars," Michael said.

"Oh shit." Frank gasped. "You're in the doghouse now."

Lainie pursed her lips, her cheeks heating. *There are a lot of people out there in need of that money. It's not only two hundred dollars. It's groceries, utilities, books, or… Stop.*

She inhaled, visualizing the beach at sunset. *Peace.*

She lifted her hand from her lap and reached forward to take a drink of her cranberry iced tea when Frank stopped her.

"The silver glow is intensifying."

Lainie looked at her wrist.

"I have no idea what is doing this. We did a lot of drawing with markers, and I worked with this idiot who used neon-colored ones. Some were silver. I noticed the glow on my wrist a little on the plane, but it went away." She looked down the top of her dress. "Dang, my chest and belly are… What the heck?"

"It's probably the marker residue showing up in this lighting," Michael said. "Don't even ask me how I know, but sometimes those markers are kind of permanent in some lighting."

"You're sensitive to medicines and oils. Maybe you've gotten a strange reaction from one of the ingredients," Frank said. "As good as it looks, it is weird."

Lainie studied the glowing oval marks. *They almost look like teeth marks. But I haven't been bitten by anything. That bizarre class and those weirdoes. I never should have taken their word about the products. I shouldn't have let them draw on me.*

"I went on a blind date a couple years ago," Michael said, interrupting her thoughts. "She was a nurse but liked to play doctor." He raised his brows and smirked. "She used some kind of neon felt-tipped pens to, uh, write on me for surgery. Some of my anatomy still glows with dotted arrows. I found some bulbs for the lights in my room that make it go away. It doesn't always show up, but for some reason, it glows around certain people and in certain lighting."

Michael picked up his drink and nearly emptied the glass.

"People?" Frank asked.

"I've never been much of a 'spiritual' kind of guy." Michael made air quotations with his fingers. "But there has to be something about certain people which give off more energy or something, 'cause I'm not kidding about that glowing stuff. It's strange."

"So what happened to the girl?" Frank asked.

"She met some artist guy and dumped my ass," Michael said. "Last I heard, she lives in suburbia and is happily married to a doctor with a kid and two dogs."

"So no one special to go home to?" Frank asked.

"Nope," Michael said. "Still looking for my mate. Uh. Soul mate."

The two men hit if off famously as they talked love, family, architecture, and homes. By the time dessert was finished, Frank had invited Michael over for lunch the next day.

The waitress handed Frank the bill.

"Let me get dinner," Michael said.

"No," Frank said. "My treat."

"Thank you," Michael said graciously. "I'll get the next one."

Jules, the owner of the restaurant, came out from the kitchen in her black chef's jacket and pulled the bill out of Frank's hand.

"You are not paying," Jules said. "Becky serenaded you, and it sounded like shit. I'm sorry. I finally get you back in, and she ruins it."

"You'll never make any money if you don't let your customers pay for their meals," Frank said.

"Kiss my ass," Jules said. "Now get out of here, or I'll tell Lainie about your latest purchase for her."

"You are no fun," Frank said. "I'm never asking your advice ever again."

"Good," Jules said. "Come back on Wednesday, and you can pay."

"He can't," Lainie stood up. "I'm cooking for him."

Frank and Michael stood up.

"I thought you were going to Chicago," Jules said.

"Nope. I canceled."

"Well then, don't look, because Eddie is coming this way." Jules stepped back and pivoted away from them.

"Fine. Run, Jules," Lainie said. "Thanks for the support." *You're not my friend. You only talk like we're tight around Frank.*

"Lainie." Eddie, the lead singer of the band she canceled on, joined them. He pulled out her chair and patted it. "Sit. Let's talk. You're nearly impossible to track down."

She sat, avoiding the hug he would attempt if she kept standing. "Fine. What?"

"Is this your husband?" Eddie held out his hand to Michael.

Michael shook his hand.

She pressed her lips together tightly.

"No, this is Michael, a friend. We're about to leave."

Eddie turned on the rock-star charm, smiled at Michael, and then glanced over at Frank.

"Hey, Frank," Eddie said. They exchanged a more elaborate and friendly handshake. "How's it going?"

They all sat down as if they were about to start cocktails. Frank and Michael were on either side of her and Eddie across from her.

"We really need you in Chicago." Eddie reached across the table and took her hands in his. "Benny's back has been killing him, and you know how Clem is dealing with his sinus issues. The pollen has been really bad lately. I need you too."

"I just got back from a trip, and I really need to stay home with my husband." She pulled her hands from his and stood up again.

The men pushed back in their chairs and stood.

She brushed Frank's arm as she stepped over to him while Michael walked around her to Frank.

"Let's get out of here before it gets crazy," she whispered. She and Frank had seen wonderful relationships and marriages fall apart under public scrutiny. They didn't want the same fate. Their marriage stayed strong. Their love continued to be protected. Keeping their private life private had been easy until Frank got sick. They found ways to keep their privacy, but it became more and more difficult.

"Don't run off." Eddie followed her. "Bring your husband. He'd probably love to hang out with us. Most guys do. We all want to meet him." He glanced at Frank and nodded. "Am I right, Frank?"

"Her husband already does get to hang out with you," Frank said. "And he doesn't want to go on tour."

"Since you're friends with him. Call and tell him how cool we are." Eddie put his arm around her husband like they were best friends. "Better yet, give me his number, and I'll surprise him. I don't want to have to follow her home."

"Don't be an asshole. Leave her alone. Go home before the cameras come out," Frank said.

"I'll leave right now, *if* you give me her husband's number," Eddie said. "Come on. We need her, man."

"Lainie's my wife," Frank shouted. "Stop being an ass."

The restaurant silenced.

"Come on." Eddie shook his head and laughed.

The man had no situational awareness.

"Just give me the guy's number," he continued. "You don't have to give me that bullshit. Look at her. She's not marrying either one of us. She's marrying a big, boring guy like the dude next to you."

"I'm not boring," Michael huffed. "Really, I'm not."

Eddie laughed and put his arm around Michael too, switching his focus from Frank.

"No offense, Mike, but I would have been surprised if you were her husband. She's too hot for a guy like you. She'd be with some big-ass fighter dude with 'killing machine' tattooed on his chest in private, but he'd be all nerdy and smart like you during the day."

The scent of woods, juniper, and marigold wrapped like a blanket around her. *Luke.*

She sighed.

Yes, Lainie. It's me. I'm coming, his voice answered her thoughts.

The wonderful desert scents of hot sand and cactus blooms mixed with the memory of Luke as the aroma grew stronger. The sensation of something tangible inside her, the one she couldn't name, vibrated warmth, comforting her.

Call me. Michael's voice interrupted her daydream, cutting off the comforting emotions and confusing the moment.

What is wrong with me? I'm imagining Luke's voice?

Michael's voice?

She slipped outside alone, lost in bemusement. Walking unnoticed past the gauntlet of paparazzi waiting for the rich and famous like Frank and Eddie, she moved to the limo.

Oh shit. Frank.

I've got him. Don't worry. Michael's voice rang in her ears.

She glanced around. She stood alone outside the commotion. Michael was nowhere near her.

Cameras flashed, lighting up the night sky.

The car door opened for her at the end of the line of photographers vying to get a good shot of them. She stopped next to the driver holding open the entrance to safety and to anonymity and gazed toward the successive bursts of lights.

Eddie posed perfectly in the middle of the action, laughing and smiling for the camera with his arm around Frank. Michael had moved to Frank's side. Her new friend's arm wrapped around Frank's back and under his arm, holding him up against the weight of the rock star. Frank and Michael smiled for the cameras as they made their way toward Frank's limo where she waited.

She slid into the car, hiding from the cameras, but when Frank, Eddie, and Michael joined her, one or maybe two flashes blinded her. She'd been caught in public for the first time.

Michael pulled the door closed.

"Dang it, Eddie," she said. "What are you doing in here?"

"Well, I didn't expect you to be here, but now that you are..." Eddie wiggled his blond eyebrows up and down. "Come on tour with me. We all like you, and you know how hard it is to find someone we all like. Let me call your husband. I'm starting to think you're not really married."

"Frank is my husband. Frank Ivanovski. The man sitting next to me. He's my husband. I'm staying home to be with him." Her blood boiled as she sat there. Frank wanted privacy. She needed privacy. "I told you when you booked me for the trip I might have to cancel last minute."

"Frank," Eddie said. "Tell me something personal about her only her husband would know."

"I'm not telling you a fucking thing, you idiot." Frank slid his hand under the hem of her dress. "We're dropping him off at his car."

"Yes, sir," the driver answered.

Eddie looked at Michael. "You knew?"

"Yeah, Lainie and I are friends," Michael said. "I'm not boring."

Eddie laughed. "You keep telling yourself that. Now Frank here, he's not boring, and he's nabbed little Lainie with the magic hands. I'm damned impressed. I'll know who to get female advice from, and it ain't you."

The limo stopped, and the door opened.

Eddie climbed out. He dipped his head back in. "Frank, I'll see you in the morning. Lainie, I'm not giving up. We need you when we go to Vegas next month."

"Not going to Vegas." *Never going to Vegas again.* "You'll have to find someone else."

Eddie's smile dropped into a flat line.

"We fight all the time unless you're there making us behave. Benny is having some trouble with his sobriety right now with all his back pain. Think about flying up after the show on Friday for a couple hours just for Benny. The rest of us won't be happy, but he really does need you."

"She'll be there," Frank said.

"No, I won't."

"She'll be there," Frank said.

"Francis Ivanovski, I told you I wasn't leaving," she yelled. She was never leaving his side again.

"Yeah, you're married to her." Eddie laughed. "See you Friday."

"No, you won't." *Get a fucking clue. Look at my husband. Take one second and really look at him.*

"She'll be there if I have to send boring Michael with her," Frank said over her objections.

"Damn it, Frank. I'm not fucking going. I'm not leaving you. Not for work. Definitely not for Eddie. Not for anyone or anything. You're not sending me away to fucking die. I won't let you. I love you more than—"

Frank pulled her against his chest. "Shh. Shh."

Whimpers bubbled up from her soul and escaped through her lips. *You can't die. You just can't. I won't let it happen.*

She slid her arms around him. "I'm not going."

"You're going." His hand drifted over her thigh, slipping under the dress. His cock hardened, pushing at her hip.

Michael cleared his throat. "I'll go with her. When is she leaving? Chicago, right?"

Having forgotten he was in the car, heat crept up her neck from the sweetness of Michael's offer and the embarrassment of him seeing the private moment between her and Frank. She buried her face against her husband's chest in an attempt to hide from her new friend.

"She leaves Thursday morning for Chicago and stays overnight. They're a bunch of rowdy boys, and she has to be there to mother hen them or—"

"They'll get crazy," Michael interrupted. "A friend of mine is supposed to come into town. Do you mind if he tags along? He's a big guy. He's a golf course designer, but back in the day, he was a self-defense instructor. He's a good guy to have around to keep boys from getting stupid."

"Sure," Frank said. "Any help Lainie can get would be great."

"Okay. Thanks."

"I'm not going," she mumbled.

"Michael, I guess I kidnapped you," Frank said. "Do you want to come over for drinks? We don't have to end the night so soon."

"Yeah, that would be great," Michael said. "I'd like to get a few more details about the trip. I'll only be a couple minutes behind you. My car is close."

"Great." Frank said.

The big man slid out of the back and closed the door.

CHAPTER TWELVE

"**D**ON'T TRY AND GET UP my skirt with company in the car." She gazed up into his beautiful blue eyes. "It was bad enough he heard us, saw us, and knows. And you invited him over for drinks? Really?" *You needed help walking to the car.*

"You're not glowing anymore." He shifted in his seat, pulling her onto his other thigh. He nuzzled the gentle curve of her neck. He slid the spaghetti straps on her shoulder down her arms.

"That's weird, isn't it?" *Could he be up for making love again?* "Do you think I could glow just around certain people?"

"Who knows?" He kissed her shoulder. "Maybe you got bitten by a vampire and don't remember. You were in Vegas. It's not called Sin City for nothing. Maybe Michael's nurse was one and fed off his dick."

She nudged him with her shoulder. "You're awful." *Are you really up for this?*

"Mmm," he whispered in her ear as his hand glided between her legs. "You love me."

"I do." She spread her legs for him. "Are you okay with this?"

Out of nowhere, he seemed better—slightly stronger. *Maybe it's a sign.*

"You know Michael is rich." His warm breath tickled her neck as his fingers inched closer to her pussy. "Not like us but pretty close."

"Does it matter?" She offered more of her hot needy flesh. She wanted him to nibble her neck like he used to. Her flesh buzzed with anticipation. *Get a little crazy and bite me all over.*

"It does matter." His tongue flicked over her throbbing pulse. "I had him checked out to make sure he wasn't a con."

"He's not." She moaned. She didn't trust most people, but Michael was different. He was genuine.

"No, he isn't." He brushed his finger over her clit, teasing her. "This afternoon he looked into buying the property west of us that crosses our road to the airport." He nipped at her neck. "I have sole rights to the road along with fifty acres of property on either side, but I haven't fenced it in. I'll make sure that is done this week."

"What is this all about?"

Humming softly, he nibbled along a musical path from her pulse to her ear. His teeth grazed across her shoulder over the place still tender from Luke's wild bite. *Luke.*

His finger slid into her creamy pussy. "Should I be jealous?"

"No, never." A flash of Luke biting her as he thrust his hard, thick cock mercilessly into her made her burn for Frank's body, his lips, his mouth, his legs, his chest rubbing against hers, his hips grinding, and his cock thrusting in and out. In and out. "Oh God."

Her fingers pulled at his pants, needing *this* Frank, the one whose desire couldn't be contained no matter how tired, how sick, or how defeated he felt. The one who could conquer any obstacle. The one who gave her hope.

"Lainie," he groaned. "Damn, baby."

She unzipped, tugged down his pants, and exposed his groin and thighs. She climbed on top of him like she had before dinner, only this time she burned to have him. She dropped down, driving his cock up into her pussy without warning.

"Bite me again," she growled into his ear. "Fuck me hard."

"Just like the very first time we ever made love." He groaned.

Her pulse quickened. Another pounding filled her ears to the rhythm of the throbbing vein at his neck.

"Yes." She growled from deep within her chest. "I wanted you so badly that night. I want you more tonight."

"That growling is fucking hot."

He grabbed the front of her dress and tore the delicate fabric down the middle. He slid it down her arms and tossed it on the floor. He pulled off his shirt and lobbed it on top of her dress. He grabbed her ass and lifted as he dropped to his knees on the clothes. He laid her back. Her shoulders and head against the leather seat on the opposite side, behind the driver.

"Wiggle those tits for me," he commanded. "And don't you hold back on me. I want your pussy squeezing my cock. I want you crazy and wild. I can take it."

She raised her hands up and shimmied her chest. His cock grew and thickened inside her as he thrust hard and fast.

"You feel like paradise." He leaned over her breast. "I should have told you to get these pierced again years ago." His tongue circled around both diamonds before his lips surrounded her breast and sucked.

"More, Frankie." Her hips bucked, countering his thrusts. Her chest arched up, pushing her full breast against his mouth.

His teeth and tongue toyed with her piercing, rolling, twisting, and pushing it back and forth. Her nipple throbbed in synchronization with her pussy's rhythmic clenching and in beat with his driving cock.

"That feels so good," she moaned.

Frank lifted his head. His beautiful blue gaze found hers.

"Yeah, it does. But I learned something new while you were gone." He locked onto her gaze and placed pressed two fingers into the depression on either side of her sacrum, accessing the reflex- ology points of her uterus, as he thrust his cock deeper into her hot sheath.

She gasped as her uterus contracted, making roll- ing waves of pleasure shoot through her pussy and up into her heart and breasts and connecting them together with love.

He ground up into a new sweet spot he discov- ered.

"I learned this one too." He thrust up into the

same spot inside her, dug his fingers into her sacrum, and slipped two fingers into her dark passage, making her pussy, ass, and womb contract. Holding her in place and refusing to let her writhe under him, he ground his pelvis in a tight semicircle, trapping her clit in a state of constant friction.

She cinched her legs tightly around his waist, attempting to take over control, but he pushed into her with more force.

"Come with me," he ordered.

She let go and exploded in bliss the second his hot liquid touched her vaginal walls.

Her pussy and dark passage clamped down, contracting against his cock in pleasurable waves, milking him of everything inside.

The weight of her worries left, her soul lifted, and her heart sang. The love of her life was going to get a miracle. Hospice would leave. She was going to have her husband strong and powerful once again.

"I think I felt the earth move," he whispered.

"Where'd you learn that?" She closed her eyes.

"One of the musicians." He pulled her along with him as he rested his butt on his heels.

"How did that come about?" She stretched and shifted her position forward. She rested her head on his shoulder and enjoyed the smooth roll of the wheels on their road.

"You know how it goes. One of the guys was talking too much about a conquest, and the rest of us were giving him shit and calling him a liar. He had to prove it, so he described a bunch of shit as we laughed. He got pissed and mentioned touching that spot and what it did…in more detail than usual. We all paid attention, still giving him shit and all, but we listened. None of us had heard about it, but we all were like, yeah, we're trying that."

She rubbed her lips against his neck. "Y'all are terrible, but that was pretty spectacular. I almost feel like I should write him a thank-you note."

"The guy should write a book about sex. He's a damned dirty dog." He rested his head against hers. "I missed you."

"I missed you too." She opened her eyes, searching for the strength, the vibrancy in his blue eyes he had minutes before. "I know you don't think we can have a baby, but what if we do? What if by some miracle we have a baby?" *It was just one night in Vegas. I don't think I can keep it a secret from you. I shouldn't have done it. But if I'm pregnant, we'll have a family. You'll have more reason to keep living and to keep fighting until there's a cure.*

"Frank, I need to—"

"Lainie…" His gaze met hers. The twinkle she'd hoped for wasn't there. The bright blue hadn't come back. The life seemed slowly fading from him. "You'll have children someday, just not with me." He swallowed, pulling her head to him. "Promise me you'll open your heart, and move on after I—"

"Shut up. No."

"Promise me."

"You're not dying. We just made love like we used to. The nurse will go home. You don't need her. You're going to have a miracle." *You have to.*

"No, I'm not." He kissed the top of her head. "You need to listen to me."

The limo stopped.

"Please." She tried to stop the ache in her heart.

She tried to stop the tide of emotions threatening to drown her. "Not today. Let me pretend we're looking forward to the future we planned together. To the family we'd have one day."

"No. You've been denying and ignoring, and you can't anymore."

Her throat constricted. "No."

His arms tightened around her. "I don't know how I had the strength to make love to you like that. I've dreamed about it for so long, but I know I'm dying. I've accepted it. You have to too."

"No, Frank. No." She moved out of his arms. "Promise me you're going to—"

"Lainie, stop." He coughed. "If you bury your head in the sand, you won't be prepared, and I need you prepared. I need to know you'll be okay. I need to know you won't go back to working all the time, not allowing anyone close to you. I need to know you'll make more than one friend every eight years."

She shook her head and stormed out of the car. Utterly naked, she stomped into the house, throwing a tantrum like a toddler. She halted in the living room. She caught a glimpse of Curtis and his grandkids exiting across the room and disappearing into the hallway. *Shit. The kids. Midnight snacks. Drinks... Michael.*

Frank caught up with her and grabbed her. His arms enveloped her, and he...stumbled.

They fell onto the couch, somehow landing on the seat cushions and missing the glass side table.

"Lainie," he panted. "Damn it." He kissed her.

The taste and scent of blood and chemicals landed on her tongue as he stroked it with his.

The pitter patter of tiny footsteps nearby echoed in the hall. The familiar, hushed giggles of children vanished as a door closed. One confident, powerful set of unfamiliar feet padded over the tile and wood floors like they were headed her way.

Frank lifted his head.

"When I'm gone, you're going to start over." Blood stained his lips.

The tidal wave of truth pulled her under, the reality of his imminent death taking her down into a riptide.

He collapsed on top of her, coughing uncontrollably. He was too heavy. Too heavy. She tried to roll him toward the back of the couch. She'd never let him fall. Never. But he was crushing her.

The ivory velvet of the fabric now was dotted with crimson stains.

"Help," she shouted. "Please, help."

Large hands pulled him from atop her. She sucked in a lungful of air and leaped from the couch.

Michael cradled Frank like a baby in his arms. "I promise I'm not into dudes. You're just too adorable not to carry."

She gazed up at Michael, biting her quivering bottom lip.

Frank lay limp in his arms, his coughing subsiding.

"I am"—he coughed, and blood trickled between his fingers—"pretty cute."

Michael strode forward, as if he'd been in their house millions of times. Straight to the bedroom where the small brunette in jeans and a T-shirt, the nurse Lainie hadn't met, sat watching television.

"He needs medical attention." Michael gently

positioned her husband in the middle of the hospital bed.

The nurse walked over and examined him, placing an IV line in his arm as Frank wheezed and coughed with every inhale and exhale. Slowly, his coughing died down, his wheezing stopped, his eyes closed, and he fell asleep.

The nurse with big brown eyes smiled the kind of apologetic smile for the pain that had come, was to come, and that which would never truly go away. Lainie had seen it before when her parents and brothers died in a car accident she should have died in too.

"I hope you had a great night out. He really wanted this to be special. It looks like you did too with all your pretty shimmering lotion," the nurse said.

Lainie opened her dry mouth.

"Uh." She swallowed, trying to get any amount of moisture to make her voice work. "It was wonderful."

She held her breath as a whimpering squeak came out.

The woman held out her hand to Michael. "Family?"

"Friend." He shook her hand. "Michael Flanagan."

"Nice to meet you." The nurse nodded. "He's going to sleep for a while."

Michael's strong arm curled around Lainie and tucked her into his side. "We need to talk."

She walked with him as he strode to the bathroom and plucked her white robe from the hook near the shower.

She slipped into the robe. She was strangely comfortable with him seeing her nude. He led her out of the bedroom through the house, entered the music room, and closed the door behind him.

"I'm sorry about tonight. I'm not going to Chicago. Don't even bother—"

"Sit," he ordered.

Her knees buckled. She went down like a lead balloon, her butt hitting the couch in a flash.

She sucked in a gasp. "What the hell?"

"We have a situation we need to talk about before you go anywhere without *me*."

CHAPTER THIRTEEN

"JUST BECAUSE YOU HELPED ME and Frank a few minutes ago doesn't mean we suddenly have a situation." She sat obediently before him, unable to get up and show him out of the house.

"We do. Frank—"

"Did Frank hire you to follow me? Befriend me?" She hadn't gotten that vibe from him, but the past twenty-four hours were anything but normal. Maybe she couldn't trust her gut anymore. She shouldn't even be here listening to him. She needed to be by her husband's side, making sure he was okay. But Frank had fallen before. All the chemo treatments, the radiation, and the biopsies had taken a heavy toll on him. Every so often he'd collapse, and she'd need help to get him to the doctor's office or hospital. She'd sit and wait, pray, cry, and pace while listening for every inhalation, every small noise, and every…

"No. It was absolute chance in our meeting. But you're lucky we did." He put his hands on his hips like he was about to *get real*. Only, she had no idea what he was going to *get real* about.

She crossed her arms and legs. He didn't seem crazy, but the neon marker story was a little unbelievable, even if she was having the same kind of reaction.

"I'm thankful you were here tonight. Thank you for not making me uncomfortable at my…um… lack of dress when you found me and Frank. But we're not that good of friends, and you're not making any sense. I'm ten seconds away from calling security, so start talking." She wasn't about to let any man walk into her home and give her orders. Maybe she had read him wrong, and he was crazy.

"You slept with a friend of mine in Vegas. The name Luke Wolfson ring any bells?"

She stopped breathing.

"I don't know a Luke Wolfson." *Is that his last name?*

Yes, Wolfson is Luke's last name, Michael's voice said in her thoughts.

She tilted her head. *Am I going crazy?*

"You're not crazy. You are going through a change at an unfortunate time in your life. We can communicate anywhere and anytime through a supernatural bond given to us by our Creator."

You're a total nut job, and you're in my house. She smiled. *Shit. How the fuck do I get your big ass out without pissing you off?*

He sighed. "You don't believe me."

"Oh no," she lied. "I believe you…" *Believe you need professional help.*

He rolled his eyes.

"I can hear you. I'm not a nut job." His brown-eyed gaze drifted to her legs as she crossed and uncrossed them. "I'm not dangerous. Just hear me out. You'll have a great story to tell everyone if you still don't believe me when I'm finished. So, just sit tight and suspend your disbelief and judgments until later."

He backed up and sat down on the opposite couch. He leaned forward, resting his hands on his enormous thighs.

Your body is so much like Frank's used be. Powerful. A deep pang filled her chest.

"I'm not just"—he smirked—"a boring finance guy. I am part of a worldwide network of men and women with a particular gene, which allows us to…" His smirk left as he inhaled deeply. "Shift, change, morph, and transform into something altogether different."

She stifled a grin. *Yep. You've got more problems than I can help you with.*

"I said 'no judgments.' I have problems, but they aren't related to who I am. They are related to who you are."

She swallowed and narrowed her focus on the handsome caramel brown of his eyes. *Repeat these words if you can hear me. I eat pinto beans, bananas, and chocolate cake.*

"Repeat these words if you can hear me. I eat pinto beans, bananas, and chocolate cake," he said and pressed his lips together in a stern yet open expression. "I'm not lying."

She nodded. She didn't know how he did it, but she'd experienced a lot of strange things over the years as a massage therapist. She was aware of the different kinds of energy that surrounded people. It was what kept her from getting close to others on a personal level. Very few people knew she was married to Frank, and the ones who did were a select few of the massage therapists she went to school with and referred clients to when she wasn't available.

He leaned back. "You're not like me, but you are."

"You don't look Native American. I've met a few over the years who had abilities I didn't understand."

"Like what?" His brows crinkled together, seemingly curious.

"Um, they could see things. Past trauma, a sickness and where it originated, and predicted events." *Frank's illness and eventual death.*

"I'm different. I actually transform. I was born this way. Ninety-nine point nine percent of us are born this way. You're different. You're human, but you have a rare compatibility with my kind. More specifically one of…" He shook his head as the energy around him seemed to turn somber.

"I'm compatible with your kind? What kind? How? What does it mean to me?"

"First, it means you met the one person you are capable of making babies with." His gaze lifted to the ceiling. "Now this is going to sound really crazy."

She half laughed. "Really crazy, huh? I'm already pretty sure this is one fucked-up dream."

He grunted a laugh. "Yeah. I never thought I'd ever meet someone like you, let alone be responsible for you in my pack."

"Pack? What are you, some kind of gang leader? I don't do gangs."

"No. You found your mate. You had sex with him.

He marked the fuck out of you. You're glowing because he went beast mode on you. Luke Wolfson is a werewolf. I'm a werewolf. In three weeks, at the full moon or maybe earlier or later. I have no idea when you'll really go through the transformation, because you're human, but it's going to happen. Oh and Luke Wolfson isn't just any werewolf. He's the biggest badass fucking Alpha in the country. He's accepting the position of Alpha over the American continents at a ceremony in his home city, Las Vegas, Nevada. He's second in line for the job of Alpha over the entire world. He's on a plane right now coming here to get you and take you home."

"Right." She huffed. "That is crazy." *I'm crazy for listening.* "We're not talking about the same man I met." *I shouldn't be admitting to even meeting someone. I never should have gone to the bar that night.*

"Green eyes, brown hair. Taller than me. Broader than any athlete you've ever seen. Strong jaw. Do you even remember the specifics of your encounter?" He raised his left brow.

"You're describing him. But he was not scary in the least."

Michael's lips spread into a wide smile.

"The more I'm around you, the more I get the sense you aren't scared of people. You're not afraid of me. You're not even worried. Why?" Michael asked.

She looked him straight in the eyes.

"I'm not afraid of you. I think you need a mental evaluation, but you're not going to harm me. Especially, since you believe some leader of"—she rolled her eyes—"your kind wants me. Seems to me it would be stupid to do anything to me unless you hate the guy, and it doesn't seem like you do."

He growled. "You don't back down. Everyone back downs to me."

"Does the big badass wolf you described back down?" She teased. *You're crazy.*

"No. He doesn't, but he respects me and my role as leader of the eastern half of the United States Werewolf Pack." His nostrils flared. "You still don't believe me."

"I'm having a hard time suspending my disbelief. If the Luke guy thinks he's a werewolf, I'm going to get some…"

Michael's jaw clenched as he pulled up the sleeve of his arm. Bristles of light brown hair popped up out of his skin. He rotated his arm inward and outward as she watched his bones crack and shift under his skin. His hands extended, his fingers grew thicker, and his hand trembled as it magically changed to a giant wolf's paw.

He grunted.

"I can continue to transform, but I'd prefer not to."

She blinked. *I can't be seeing this.*

"You are, Lainie. You're seeing the arm of my wolf."

She stood up and walked over to him. "May I touch your arm?" *This isn't possible.*

"Yes." He held out his paw.

She gazed into his eyes as she held his paw. Her fingers slid over the silky fur and calloused pads of his paw. Gliding between each pad, over his claws, and up along the arm until his shirt cut off the rest.

"I'm going to do this?"

"No. You won't have control. You'll go through a

full and quite painful transformation into a wolf."

She massaged over his shirt across his shoulder and neck. "It looked painful, but you didn't cry. Did your bones actually break? They looked like they broke and reformed."

"I'm used to the change. I've been doing it for hundreds of years."

"Hundreds?"

"Yes. You'll have a long life and look exactly the same for eternity after your first Shift. Your wolf won't be fully formed for a year maybe? I'm not sure. You're different than us. We don't stop aging until our beasts mature. Some stop aging in their late teens. Others don't stop until they are gray. I've stopped, and so has Luke."

"You can save my husband. Go bite him. Do it now." She grabbed his paw and pulled as she took a step.

"No. It doesn't work like that." His hand rippled underneath her grip. Bones shifted. Fur receded.

She let go of him and backed up. "Oh my God."

"Your husband is not like you. He doesn't carry the marker you do. He's not compatible. I could bite him to kill him, but I can't save his life. He's going to die within a week."

"Get out of my house." Heat burned her cheeks. "In all the movies, werewolves bite a person, and that person becomes a werewolf."

"Yeah. That's the movies. It's not real life. This is real life. You're turning into a werewolf because you found your mate, went through a mating heat along with a mating bond, and now you're pregnant and mated. You belong to Luke Wolfson, and he has every right to come and take you home with him. The only person stopping him is me. Me. That's it. You'll probably go back in a trance as soon as you touch him." He slapped his hands to his face and rubbed.

"I was never in a trance." *Was that how my luggage got in the room? No. I was drunk. I was drunk, not in any trance.*

He raised his hands in the air. "Why me? Why the fuck did I have to be on the same plane as you? I couldn't leave well enough alone. I had to like you. I had to feel your wolf crying. I had to follow up. Why, God, why?"

His ears grew and sprang fur.

"Uh, your ears, Michael. They're dog ears."

"*Wolf* ears. I'm not a domestic dog. I'm a fucking Alpha wolf."

"Yeah, okay. I believe you. You can stop now."

His mouth and nose extended. The rip of cartilage and crack of bones under his skin that went along with his transformation made her cringe, but she watched anyway, surprisingly curious at the change. *How is this even possible?*

He shook his head back and forth like a wet dog drying off, then stopped. His face inexplicably had turned back to picture-perfect normal. "Do you believe me now?"

She nodded. "Yes, sir."

"Good. I'm your Alpha. I've got men from my pack guarding your house. I'll be back before the sun rises. Luke will not step foot on your property until we're ready—meaning until I've got safeguards in place. I can't control him everywhere, but I can stop him from entering *my territory.*"

"Yes, sir."

"I'm sorry about your husband. We're going to figure this out. I'm here. You can lean on me."

She turned away from him and walked out of the room like she had when she found out Frank's cancer was terminal.

You're going to have to work on respecting your Alpha. His voice rang in her head.

Respect is earned. Please don't let Luke come here. I don't want my husband to know what I've done. I wanted a baby and a family with my husband. I wanted to give him another reason to live. I just wanted one night of love. One night to make a miracle happen. One measly night with a stranger. Nothing more.

CHAPTER FOURTEEN

LAINIE PLOPPED DOWN ON THE purple velvet armchair in her massage room on the southwestern side of the house. All she wanted was a little privacy from everyone to calm down and breathe. With the tale Michael had told her last night and repeated that morning, she wasn't sure what to or not to believe.

"We need to talk," Michael said.

Startled, she bolted up to standing and turned around to the sound of his voice. "What are you doing here?"

"Good morning to you too," Michael said, standing inside the room, blocking her exit. "This is my brother Gabriel."

At first glance, the two men looked identical, wearing black basketball shorts and red athletic T-shirts, but on closer inspection, Michael's eyes were a darker brown, and his hair had red undertones while his brother's eyes were a light amber and his dark hair had golden hues sprinkled throughout.

"I'm sorry about last night and earlier this morning. I didn't want to spring so much on you all at once," Michael said.

"Is he one?" She didn't want to assume anything ever again. She had assumed she'd have one night with Luke and be gone, never to be heard from again. She had been wrong.

"Yes. He's in Luke's pack."

She nodded. "Right. Of course he is." *I should have had sex with the blue-eyed guy at the bar, and I wouldn't be in this mess.*

"That's Danny," Gabriel said. "And you're right. You wouldn't be pregnant. Danny would be dead. Luke would have killed him, and you would be in a worse situation."

She held up her hand.

"I don't need this from you. If you're trying to blackmail me for money, just do it. My husband is dying, and I've got my head on straight now. Your silly tale and illusion trick are over. You need to go." *I'm not exhausted and overwhelmed anymore. I can think rationally.*

"Are we back to questioning my integrity?"

"No, no. I get it. The lotion isn't making me glow. It's you and possibly"—she pointed to Gabriel—"you."

She walked to the dresser near the door and grabbed a set of sheets to keep busy. She doubted Frank would leave his bed today. But, if he changed his mind and wanted a massage, the room would be ready.

"The Alpha from France will be here in a couple hours. Her name is Zoe," Michael said.

"Tell her to go home. I'll deal with whatever is or isn't happening to me on my own." *I don't care what's happening to me. I need Frank to get better.*

She placed the sheets on the wooden stool at the head of the massage table and began dressing it.

Michael strode to her. He took hold of one side of the sheet and helped her fit the edges over the corners.

"I've never been in a situation like this," he said. "There hasn't been a werewolf-compatible human in more than five hundred years. Long before I was born. You're rare."

She nodded.

"Yes. I had the unfortunate experience of unknowingly fucking a werewolf. Now, I'm glowing where he bit me." She gazed up at the glow-in-the-dark stars Frank painted on the ceiling three years ago hoping one day there would be reason to turn it into a nursery. "But the glitter only appears around other werewolves. Now, because of sex and biting, I'm going to live for, well, forever. But, it's only because I'm rare. I can't bite Frank and save him or help him live forever because he's not compatible. It's really convenient for you to save me and not him. Right? Works into your sick world."

"I'm going to wait outside for Zoe," Gabriel said. "Nice meeting you, Lainie." His gaze darted around the room. "If there's something I can do to help, I'm here."

"You're not going to go furry on me and run around the house on four legs, are you?" She didn't mean to be so argumentative, but she couldn't stop. *I don't want to live forever without Frank. I don't want to live at all.*

Gabriel halted, glanced in Michael's direction,

and leaned his back against the wall. His progression out of the room seemed to be on hold for a while.

Placing her hand flat on her table, she let her head hang down as the weight of despair overwhelmed her.

"I probably will go all furry, ma'am," Gabriel said. "It's easier. It's why we're wearing shorts and T-shirts. We can get naked easily and dress quickly."

She squeezed her lids closed. "I'm sorry."

"It's okay. I figured you'd be scared of us, but you're not. I'm sorry about your husband. Michael introduced me to him. I'm just sorry. He's really great when he's not unconscious."

"Thanks. It's the medicine. It's too much."

"It's not," Gabriel said softly. "He's in a tremendous amount of pain. You are too."

Her throat squeezed shut as if she were being choked. She struggled to swallow as her eyes welled with tears. She wasn't falling apart. Her husband needed her.

After a few tries, she pushed down the real fear driving her into the ground. Losing him would be too much. But, if Michael was right, she was going to have a baby. The baby she'd prayed for since the first time she and Frank had made love. The baby who never came until she was so desperate to give her husband a new reason to fight, to live, and to believe in miracles.

"I lived on a farm growing up. Life and death went hand in hand… Do go hand in hand." Frank in that hospital bed in their bedroom was not the way things were intended. "When I met Frank…" She inhaled the scent of whiskey. "He smelled like a triple shot of the richest whiskey a person could buy. The energy around him buzzed. People flocked to him, still do, even now. He always says it was a blind date, but it wasn't. I refused to go out with him the first time he asked."

"That doesn't surprise me," Michael mumbled.

"He took my phone and programmed his number in it."

"A player," Gabriel said.

She lifted her head and sat down on the edge of her massage table. "Yeah. He texted me song lyrics every day for a month. I had to get rid of him, so I finally accepted a dinner date. I had no idea who he was. I didn't care. I was a struggling massage therapist with six dogs in a one-bedroom apartment. I was looking forward to not paying for dinner."

"So why were you mad when he brought you to a nice restaurant?"

"I was dressed in jeans and a T-shirt. He was in a suit. I came from a one-restaurant town, and it was fast food. I didn't even think he'd take me somewhere fancy. We argued like cats and dogs. He kept telling me I looked beautiful and no one would say a word about my clothes."

"Did anyone say anything?" Gabriel asked.

"No. No one even noticed me. Everyone was after him. Slipping him flash drives. Handing him business cards." She smiled. *He was so polite and generous and humble. Tall. Strong. A force to be reckoned with.*

"So what changed?" Gabriel asked.

"He tackled her," Michael said. "Like a beast."

"No. That wasn't it. I was done even after that,

but he wasn't. We ended up at a fast-food joint. No one paid attention to us. We shared burgers and fries and even sundaes. Then, he took me home. He walked me to my apartment door and asked if I liked the lyrics he sent me."

"Did you?" Gabriel asked.

"No. I didn't, and I told him so. I unlocked my door and was about to turn the doorknob when he whispered, 'Give me one more date. Listen to the song I'm sending you tonight. Please, just take one listen. If you don't love the song, then you won't love me as much as I already do you.' My heart did weird things when he got so close to me. I opened the door and hurried into my apartment like a coward."

"No kissing?" Gabriel asked.

She shook her head. "But no more than ten minutes later, he sent me a song he sang and wrote that nearly tore my heart out. And that was when I knew there was no one else I'd ever love the way I love him. We went on a second date and got married on the third in my parents' house in my hometown. Just my small family and his best friend."

"He's a smart guy," Gabriel said. "Luke is smart too. You don't know much about him, but we do. He's—"

"I don't care about him. The only man I care about is lying in bed doped up on morphine. He's talking about working today, and he can't even get up without Curtis. I'm not strong enough to help him."

Michael slid across the table and pulled her into his lap. He embraced her. "There is a reason for everything. You're going to get through this, and we have to make plans for your trip to Chicago."

She curled her body around his like she had done as a child with her daddy. "I'm not leaving Frank."

"He wants you to go. He has a surprise he's planning, and you have to be out of the house," Michael said. "Not going isn't an option."

"I'm not going." *Frank will not get his way this time.*

"Baby werewolf throwing a tantrum?" a female voice she didn't recognize said.

Michael growled.

"Zoe, can you act like you care just a little? With all the sensitivity-training shit you're making us do, I'd think you could use the skills you're teaching everyone."

"That's for Luke and only Luke. Until he can stand in a room full of Alphas and at least act like he cares, I'm bound to keep doing the fucking workshops for all the Alphas. *You try* and teach him about cellphone etiquette without pissing him off. You try and find new ways to talk about sensitivity to an Alpha who has virtually none. Two hundred and fifty years I've been forced to deal with him, and now I'm stuck doing workshops titled 'Sensitivity Training' he only thinks is for the weak. So she needs to get used to it. She's already mated to the asshole. God, she stinks. This fucking house stinks of death and *him*."

Lainie pushed free from Michael to see the audacious woman daring to insult her, her husband, and her…*mate.*

"Who do you think…?" Lainie stopped in front of the woman.

The long-haired blonde beauty before her tilted

her head and stuck her lips out as if she were posing for a duck-face selfie.

"I'm an Alpha," Zoe said, nodding as if Lainie was too stupid and slow to understand her. "You're a weak little human with a weak little werewolf trying to grow big enough to transform. Oh, and you're carrying Luke's pup inside you. Get your suitcase and your ass in my rental, so I can get the angry Luke Wolfson off my fucking back."

Lainie straightened her spine and got in the angelic face of the runway model bitch. "Here's an idea. Get the fuck out of my house and go back to whatever fashion show you came from."

Zoe grabbed Lainie's neck. "I could kill you right now."

"But then, you'd never get Luke Wolfson off your fucking back."

"Actually, if you die, he does too. The beauty of a werewolf mating. Only you're an unknown in this factor, *human*. Michael knows if I kill you and lover boy Luke lives, I'm dead. I'm sure that is the only reason he called me in for help." She shoved Lainie back, releasing her.

Lainie stumbled into Michael. *Bitch. Is this werewolf thing that serious? I don't want Luke to die because we spent… Mmm. His hands. His mouth.*

Lainie, Luke's voice filtered into her thoughts. *You're going to get down on your knees and suck my cock. You're going to bite me, marking me in the old ways. I'm going to reward you. I'm going to lick your pussy, rub my face in your sweet peaches. I'm going to shove my cock inside you and make you come so hard, sweetheart. So. Fucking. Hard.*

She slid her hand down her jeans. *Yes, Luke. I'm*

going lick you, taste you, swallow your cock, and suck. You'll have your mouth on my clit…

Her fingers glided back and forth over the swollen bead. *Lick it, Luke. Graze your teeth over the hard wet nub. Please. Do it, Luke.*

And it was as if his hand were at her clit, rubbing, not hers. And his tongue she sensed licking between her legs, not her fingers swiping along and dipping into her swollen and drenched pussy.

"Damn, he's good," Zoe said. Her voice shattered the connection. "But he's losing control over his mental pack filters. First order of business. No bond communication until she's turned. Human contact only. There are only two documented human turned werewolves recorded in our history. Both were women. Both died during their first fight. Things don't look good for you. But things are looking damned good for me."

"She's going to survive," Michael said. "You don't know her."

"And you do?" Zoe huffed. "You're thinking like Luke—with your dick. Take one hard look at her. She's submissive. She's weak. She's pining over a guy who is three-quarters of the way under the azaleas. And she's a pampered princess to boot. She's not a fighter. She's a girl who lies down and shows her belly to the stronger player. Luke couldn't have picked a bigger loser."

"Since I'm that big of a loser, leave. I'm not going anywhere. I'm staying right here."

"With your hand down your pants?" Zoe turned away from her and walked toward the door.

Son of a…bitch. Lainie removed her hand from her jeans. "What happened to your shoes? Broke a heel? Couldn't find a color wheel to help you match?"

Zoe turned on a dime and rushed at her.

Lainie stepped aside at the last second, making the blonde collide with Michael.

"Good job, *Grace*," Lainie said. "I'm surprised you've got any kind of leadership status when you can barely walk on your own feet." She pressed her finger to her mouth and tapped, as she gazed at the stars on the ceiling. "Oh, wait. What do you call yourselves? Hmmm? Alpha?"

A low rumble came from the pissed-off blonde. The wooden planks vibrated under Lainie's feet. "I won't miss next time, *human*."

"Whatever." Lainie walked to the door. "Michael, I'll see you later."

"We need to talk," Michael said.

"No. We don't. Get the bitch out of my house. I don't need her bullshit. Tell Luke to go away. I'm not dealing with him either."

"No." Michael growled. "You don't get this situation. Luke is not going away."

"Yes, he is," she said.

"Luke will take you to the ground and fuck you into submission if he has to," Michael said.

"He will not," Lainie said.

Michael quickly grabbed her arm and swung her around to face him. "If we don't start a dialog with him now, he's going to break into this house, and—"

"If he does, I'll have his ass arrested and dump him in jail," she said.

Zoe laughed. "That would be a first."

Michael sighed. "He can help you through this

stuff with Frank."

"No, he can't. No one can." She tugged her arm free and walked out of the room, leaving the door ajar to eavesdrop.

"Good one, bro," Gabriel said. "Luke is coming, and she doesn't even acknowledge you as her Alpha. Frank is her Alpha, and he's not even a werewolf."

"She's fragile right now," Michael said. "Curtis told me she's been roaming the house sleepwalking and sobbing for months."

"Luke could help with that," Gabriel said.

"Did you say she's mated with the other human?" Zoe asked.

"Yes," Michael said. "The mating bond scent is under the smoke and ash."

"That isn't possible," Zoe said. "Humans don't do that."

"Well, she did. And, if she doesn't show me she can control her emotions, I'm going to have to bring her to my house and cage her."

"That thing?" Zoe said. "Caged?"

"Watch her run. Humans don't run like that. If she Shifts without Luke to control her, I'm going to need help and not just from you. The World Alpha is involved."

"World Alpha?" Zoe's voice squeaked.

"Yes." His voice rose. "My newest pack member ran from Luke after they mated. No one leaves their mate, especially humans. Her husband will be dead in a few days. I don't know how the hell he's still alive, working, talking, and fucking breathing."

Lainie hurried down the hall, afraid to hear any more. She had paced most of the night, and then Michael had shown up around two in the morning, joining her. He talked her ear off. Repeated the dangers of not being with Luke. Repeated the going-furry issue. Repeated the inevitable death of her husband and move to Nevada. He repeated and repeated and repeated until the consequences of her actions were embedded in her brain.

She entered the bedroom and headed straight to her husband. The nurse administered more morphine to him.

"Stop that. He's unconscious." She pulled the sunburst orange blanket covering her husband up to his chin.

"Mrs. Ivanovski, I'm here to make his last days comfortable. You and I can discuss this somewhere else."

"You're doping him up," she shouted. *I am coming unglued. Michael's right. I have to pull it together. But my husband doesn't need all that shit in his system.* "Am I the only one who is seeing this?"

"I'll get the doctor on the phone for a conference." The woman pressed her lips together into a thin-lined smile as she picked up her phone from the side table.

"Good." Lainie stomped out of the bedroom and down hall, catching sight of the blonde bitch with Michael and Gabriel stepping into a guest bedroom. *I need to calm down, or he will put me in a damn cage. The nurse would be glad to get rid of me.*

The nurse quietly closed the door to the master suite and took the lead, walking down the hall.

Lainie followed her, getting more irritated with every step. By the time they arrived in the living room and sat down on the couch, her skin itched, and her mind raced with ways to get the woman and everyone else out of her home.

The nurse held her cell phone between them.

"I'm here with Mrs. Ivanovski."

"Lainie," Dr. Collins said. "Can you hear me?"

"Yes, Dr. Collins. Frank is being overmedicated. How can he fight the disease if he's doped up all the time?"

"Have you called the support group I told you about?" Dr. Collins asked. "Frank has accepted what is happening to him. Have you accepted it?"

Lainie's mouth dropped open, and she fell back into the couch, limp. *What should I accept? As long as he's living, there's a chance of a miracle.*

"Lainie," Dr. Collins said. "Are you still there?"

"Mrs. Ivanovski?" The woman patted her hand.

"Mrs. Ivanovski, we talked about end care during the last visit," Dr. Collins said.

"This can't be happening." *I need everyone to believe he will make it.*

"He wants these last days to be as pain free as possible…" The nurse continued speaking while Lainie's mind raced to find a way out of the nightmare. *Frank. Luke. Werewolves. Eternity. Death. Death. Death.* "I'm here for you too," the woman said.

Exhaling slowly, Lainie focused on the things she could control, like her mind and her actions.

The woman squeezed Lainie's hand. "You're going to get through this. It seems like you won't right now, but things will get better."

"They told me that the day my parents and brothers died. They said it would take some time to heal. It's been seven years. It still hurts. So, don't tell me I'm going to get through this. Frank is my everything. I'm never going to heal from this. I'm never getting over it."

There has to be a way I can turn him into a werewolf and make him live forever. There has to be a way to save him. I'll do anything to save him.

"Mrs. Ivanovski," the woman continued. "There are women in the support groups who have been where you are now. They've survived, healed, and moved on the way their loved ones wanted. You will too."

She jerked her hand from the nurse. "You don't know a damned thing about me, so don't act like you do. The only thing anyone can say to me that will make me heal is, 'there was a mistake,' and he's not dying."

She stood up and faced the pretty brunette with big brown eyes seemingly radiating sympathy.

"So, thanks for trying, but I don't need you patting my fucking hand or telling me a support group will get me through this. As soon as Frank's gone, you'll have moved on, and I'll be…" *Lost. Alone. Dying inside.*

All the oxygen seemed to be sucked from her lungs. Her legs trembled. Her heart stopped beating. The darkness she'd always courted in her younger years. The darkness of the man she'd been with, before she met Frank, chased back into the depths of her soul, and kept it from surfacing. The darkness her dogs protected her from. The darkness Frank had destroyed with his love was back, creeping closer to taking over her thoughts, clawing at her to let go of all control so it would rule her.

Blinking back the tidal wave of emotions smashing against the surface, she labored to breathe. *He can't die. I can't live without him.*

"Yell and scream," the nurse said softly. "I can take it. But nothing is going to change the fact your husband's time on earth is almost over."

"Don't." Lainie raised her hands and turned her head away from the nurse. "I'm going to get him a miracle. I'm going to find a way to heal him. He's not going to die."

There is no miracle, Michael's voice echoed in her mind. *He's already halfway to the other side.*

On shaky legs, she walked out of the room and down the hall. The scent of death overwhelmed her as she entered the bedroom.

Smoke.

Ash.

Death.

CHAPTER FIFTEEN

THE LOVE OF HER LIFE slept in the bed. The breathing mask pumped air into his lungs. The *drip, drip, drip* of the IV fluids into the line. The constant buzzing from the exhausts incessantly forcing the stagnant air out of the house. All the things she'd never noticed before, she noticed now.

Your wolf is growing, Michael whispered in her thoughts.

I don't want to hear you in my head. I don't want to think about you or it. I hate you. I hate your kind.

She laid her head down and sniffed Frank's neck. *Death.*

"I love you."

With a medicated glaze over his eyes, Frank slowly lifted his hand to his mouth and pulled the mask to the side. "I love you. I'm going to rest for a little bit. Dirty Dog is coming over, and I'm going to be in the studio with him later."

Dirty Dog wasn't coming to work. He was coming with some of his friends to visit. Frank hadn't been in the studio working yesterday. He'd lied to her. He'd been resting, making phone calls, and telling his closest friends about his illness.

"Okay."

"Lainie," Curtis shouted from the hallway. "There is a Zoe Geroux here to see you. She's with the grief support group. You're running together?"

Oh God. No.

She kissed Frank's neck and forehead and adjusted his oxygen mask back in place. He'd already fallen back asleep.

She climbed off the bed and hurried to the hallway. Zoe stood a few feet behind Curtis. Her presence took up more space than the average person.

Lainie looked up at Curtis. His bloodshot eyes and trembling lips hit her in the gut and made her belly churn.

"There really is no hope, is there?"

He avoided her eyes and shook his head. "I'm going sit with him for a while. Please talk to Zoe. I feel like I'm going to lose you too, and that is too much for a man like me."

She nodded. Her vocal cords seemed to calcify, refusing any attempt to make a sound.

Zoe strode to Lainie's side.

"I'm going to take him into the studio for a bit," he continued. "Ricky is here finishing up a few songs Frank wanted on the album."

Lainie nodded.

"Let's go. It's a beautiful morning for a run." Zoe's fingers threaded between hers.

Like a robot, Lainie followed her outside to the Olympic-size track Frank had insisted on building her.

"Hurdles. Javelin. Discus throw. High jump. Long

jump. Shot put. Pole vault. Do you actually do any of those, or are they for show?" Zoe asked.

"I do. My dad was a decathlete and an archer in high school. He made it to state in both. There is an indoor archery range at the back of the property. It's been a while since I've practiced."

"Are you any good at any of it?" Zoe narrowed her gaze, pissing Lainie off completely.

"I was an alternate on the Olympic archery team. What about you?"

"I run. I'm the best female fighter of our kind in the world. Do you fight?"

"No." *Not since I lost it on the kindergarten playground and beat the shit out of Peter Vick for hitting my dog with a rock.* "I'm a massage therapist. We're lovers, not fighters. Peace. Relaxation. Acceptance. Love. I'm into that."

"Your husband will be dead in less than a week. Accept it."

I know. I fucking know. Why won't anyone let me pretend?

"Because you're making it impossible for everyone around you, especially your husband. Humans die. They die all the time. They're fragile."

"Fuck you."

"Here are the facts. The second your husband takes his last breath or you shift into a wolf, Luke will be here. He will take you. Because Luke will be Alpha over all werewolves on this continent. The strongest female, Chrissy Clemmons, will most likely be the first to challenge you. Chrissy will take advantage of your pregnancy. She will fight to kill you, which will be easier than it should be because your wolf won't be fully grown for another year."

"So, your point is what?"

"I have been elected to hold the unlucky position of being over all werewolf-compatible humans who have mated. You're my first. So, human, I'm responsible for keeping your ass alive. I'm testing your skills today. You're going to run, and I'm going to chase you for an hour."

"I'm doing sets of sprints and the javelin throw today." She walked over to the equipment Curtis already set out for her in the middle of the track field. "Join me or run. Whatever you want, but you're on my schedule. My house. My rules."

Zoe growled. "You better learn some respect."

"Or what?"

"I'll teach you some."

Lainie picked up the first javelin. "Why would the fight end in my death? I thought werewolves are damned near impossible to kill."

"Chrissy wants to move up the chain of command. It's hard to get a promotion, and she's not patient. If she eliminates you, she eliminates Luke. We can regenerate cells at an incredible rate. We can regrow limbs. But, if you sever the spinal cord, remove our heads, and rip out the heart, it's pretty much over."

"What if I refuse to fight?"

"She kills you. Luke dies. I lose respect, and Chrissy might come after me for my position. She'll bring war to the different packs. Peace will most likely be a thing of the past."

Lainie breathed in and focused on the farthest white line in the distance.

The intense rays of the sun heated her muscles

and warmed them. She should have run a few laps to get rid of some of the excess emotional energy she carried.

"You're weak. You're a submissive little bitch. You're a fucking human piece of shit…"

Lainie ignored the woman's ranting and raised the javelin as she started the routine her father ingrained in her. *The sky. The earth. The moon. The sun. All work in the way God created them. I come from cosmic dust. Anything is possible. Breathe in the celestial energy. Let it flow through my veins. I am light. I am powerful.*

Her hand released the rod. The momentum carried it over the lush grass. It landed exactly where she targeted—the outer corner of the white line. She walked over and picked up another javelin.

"Listen to me," Zoe shouted.

She glanced over her shoulder at the red-faced blonde. "This is my time. It's the only peace I have. Go away."

"I'm going to end this stupidity and kill your husband."

Lainie's gums tingled, and her heart raced. Her hand gripped the sharpened rod.

"You so much as walk near him, and I'll kill you." She growled. "I'll swim in your blood and put your fucking head on a damned spike in my driveway."

The woman fluffed her hair and smiled. "I see sensitivity training in your future. I'll leave you alone. For now."

"Ah," she screamed. "Get out."

"We're going to be besties. There's something about you, little pup." Zoe stuck her tongue out at her. "You're going to make Luke absolutely crazy. I can't wait." She walked over to the inner track and stretched.

Instead of throwing the javelin at Zoe, she turned around and stared off at the tall Georgia pines shading Curtis's house.

I'll never give up on you, Frank. Two weeks ago we talked about having a family. About going on a vacation. Yesterday, we made love twice. You're tired. You did too much yesterday. You're going to get a cure.

Yesterday, he had the rally before the death call, Zoe whispered in her mind. *You're supposed to have peace afterward. Only somehow you mated him like a werewolf, and that doesn't alleviate the pain. It amplifies it. I've never seen anyone mated survive their mate's death. But for some very strange reason, I believe you will not only survive, but thrive.*

Lainie dropped her javelin. *I don't want to survive his death.*

Yes, you do. It's why you followed your instincts to leave your terminally ill husband and fly to Las Vegas for a miracle. You're desperate to survive.

CHAPTER SIXTEEN

LUKE WALKED AMONG THE HUSTLE and bustle of activity along the Magnificent Mile in Chicago, waiting for Lainie to arrive in the city. Gabriel let it slip to Danny, Luke's Beta, that Michael had made sudden plans to go to Chi-Town, and where Michael went, so did Lainie. The man would not let Lainie out of his sight until she was delivered to Luke. That was one fact they both agreed upon. Finally, Luke had a chance to track her down and bring her home.

My mate.

His body thrummed with excitement to see her again, to be close, and to rub every inch of his body all over her sexy curves.

His beast pushed at him to get free. No contact with her except through human means was killing him. He wasn't allowed to enter Atlanta or its suburbs. Michael had brought in Zoe Geroux, France's female Alpha, and convinced her to help with Georgia's newest pack member—the human, Elaine Ivanovski.

Trying to beat Michael at his own game, Luke

had called in help from the top, World Alpha Dietrich Wolfgang. But no, the man wouldn't intervene when Zoe Geroux was involved. On top of that, Lainie was a woman and a human. Mr. World Alpha himself washed his hands of the situation. That left Luke to work with Michael and Zoe to get his mate, bending pack rules to fit his needs and reminding them when he took over as World Alpha after Dietrich retired, things would be different.

Secrets didn't sit well with Luke. He didn't like being out of the loop, but the lengths to which Michael had gone to eliminate any contact with her until later in the month told him Lainie needed him now, not later.

Taking this trip was a gamble, but Michael knew he was in the area.

The scent of peaches, peanuts, and pine mixed with his scent of juniper, marigold, and sunshine blew in from the southeast. *My Lainie.*

His cock twitched. His ears perked up, and he tamped his wolf down. She was here, but why? Was she really a massage therapist? He wasn't so sure. Nothing popped up anywhere he looked about her work or private life. He was starting to think she was one of those off-the-grid people. *But she would smell like gunpowder, lead, dirt, and fear. My mate doesn't carry any of those scents.*

He'd been stopped by Zoe at the Atlanta airport earlier in the week and forced back on a plane returning to Las Vegas. Zoe thwarted his plans to get his mate and bring her home. He had to trust Michael. Whatever serious situation his mate was in, she needed him with her. Fucking diplomacy.

He missed the old days when he'd just tear apart anyone between him and his goal.

His nostrils flared. His beast breathed in more of the scent, tracking her to Soldier Field before her scent faded away. He inhaled her scrumptious aroma calling to him. He basked in it, closed his eyes, and filled his mind with her lovely blue eyes, her luscious lips, and her luminous light caramel hair with golden highlights.

He sighed. *Mine.*

Taking in more of her through his nose, he caught another scent and growled. *Peaches, pine trees, cactus blooms, and sand. Michael Flanagan.*

He forced the other Alpha's scent from his lungs. Only Lainie's mattered. *Peaches, peanuts, and pine mixed with marigold, juniper, and sunshine. I will see you tonight, my beautiful mate.*

He strode down the street, as people moved to the sides allowing him a direct line toward the stadium. A sold-out concert for a local band that made it big was scheduled to play at the stadium later that night. But why was she there? Was she friends with the band? Massaging them? Promoting them? Why the hell wouldn't Michael or Zoe divulge any information on his mate?

He stopped tracking her and entered the hotel he was staying in. If he scented Michael, then Michael had to have scented him. He would have to make contact and give his updated itinerary. Mediation sucked.

Back in the hotel room, he bought an outrageously priced ticket online to the rock concert and changed his clothes. One last chance to make a good impression, he checked himself out in the mirror. A green athletic-cut T-shirt with black swirls showed off his muscular chest.

Yeah, she's going to love it. She won't be able to resist me. She'll run to me as soon as she sees me. She'll attack me.

A rumble started in his chest and lifted to his throat, forming a deep satisfied growl.

Yeah, she's going to attack me, giving me every right to take her home with Michael's blessing. She'll beg to leave with me.

He left his hotel room and headed down to the lobby.

The buzz in the glitzy gold-and-crystal atrium was about the concert he was going to and the hot lead singer, Eddie Chance. He smiled as several teens squealed every time the man's name was mentioned.

He strode to the concierge for information on the band and to get a limo for the night.

His ears perked up when one of the older girls in front of him at the concierge counter said the band had brought a massage therapist on tour because the drummer had been dealing with back pain. The girl continued telling her friend she was going to massage school in Arizona after high school to tour with bands, actresses, actors, and celebrities like the one Eddie Chance hired.

"May I help you?" The tall redheaded concierge interrupted his eavesdropping.

"I'm going to the concert tonight." He asked about the band, but she was little to no help, just stating it was going to be a great show. "I need a limo immediately."

She handed him her business card with her cell

number written on the back. "The black limousine with the driver holding the number four is waiting for you. If you need anything else, call me."

"Thank you." He smiled at the woman shushing the two female teens that he'd been eavesdropping on and then stopped. He turned around. "Did I hear you're going to the concert tonight?"

"Yes," the woman said. "Hoping to catch a cab before the concert starts. But the line is out of sight."

"I'm going. You and the girls can ride with me," he offered. "I'm supposed to meet a friend there, but I think she's going to stand me up."

The woman, a cute brunette, looked him up and down.

He wasn't used to such a blatant ogling, but as long as the girls got in the car and blabbed everything they knew about the massage therapist touring with the band, he'd deal with it.

"Believe me, she's not standing you up." She exhaled. She shook her head and slouched. "Sorry." She squared her shoulder and gazed into his eyes. "Yes, we'd love to catch a ride with you."

The girls hugged each other, then hurried over to Luke.

"So, what's your name?" asked the tiny brunette who looked like the adult with them but had a slightly different scent. Possibly the woman's niece? "I'm Sara."

"And I'm Kara, Sara's friend," the little blonde said. "Usually, Sara and I—"

"Finish each other's sentences," Sara said.

"I'm Mere, Sara's mom," the woman said.

You're not biologically her mother, but you are related.

"I'm Luke Wolfson. It's nice to meet you." He escorted the giggling girls out of the hotel on one arm and the mom on the other.

Mere slid into the back of the limo.

The girls climbed in and sat in the black leather bench seat opposite Mere.

He talked to the driver for a minute and climbed in. The girls spread out across the entire length of the seat behind the driver's section as soon as he entered.

He sat next to the young mom, who was wearing jeans and a black T-shirt.

Mere smiled. There was a flash of a camera. She looked with daggers in her eyes over at her daughter.

Sara bit her bottom lip and shrugged innocently.

"I had to. I'm recording the trip for posterity. Plus, he's totally cute for an old guy."

Mere's face turned bright red. "Girls, behave."

"He's got to be thirty," Kara said. "That's almost as old as you."

He chuckled. *If they only knew how old I really am.*

"I'm thirty-one," Luke said. "I don't think that's old, but I'll take it as a compliment."

Mere inhaled and faced him.

"I'm sorry. Teenagers are, well, teenagers." She raised her hands, opened her palms, and dropped them on her lap. "Sorry."

"Don't worry about it. I want to hear about the band. I paid an arm and a leg for the ticket and don't know much about them."

"The band is really good. We've had tickets for a long time, but I'm here for a job too," Mere said.

"The band has a massage therapist who is amazing," Sara said. "Mom took a class with her. They're close friends. And now I'm going to see Eddie Chance in person." Sara bounced up and down, holding Kara's hand.

"They have a massage therapist?" he asked. *It has to be Lainie.*

"They do," Mere said. She lowered her chin and glanced over at Sara. Immediately Sara stopped bouncing and sat up straight. Mere raised her chin and continued. "Lainie and I went to massage therapy school together. She's unbelievably good and even refers me business sometimes. Well, like now."

"Now?" he leaned back in the seat, although he wanted nothing else but to use his Alpha power to make her tell him everything immediately.

Her gaze lowered to her hands, and her bright expression faded to gray.

"She's had a really hard year. She asked if I would replace her for this tour. She's helped me out so many times over the years. I'd like to take this burden off her hands."

"And I'll get to go on tour too," Sara said, grabbing her friend's arm and shaking it.

"So what has changed?" *She wouldn't have to cancel her business obligations when she moved in with me unless I was unavailable to go with her. I'd move mountains to make her happy.*

"It's personal. Sad. Very sad. My heart breaks for her. She's suffered enough in her life. She doesn't need what's happening now."

His heart stopped. Whatever she was alluding to with Lainie had nothing to do with him. "I hate to pry, but what is going on with her?"

"I… Are you a psychologist or something? I just

want to keep talking, and I can't."

He shook his head.

Just part of being Alpha. Now tell me everything you know about my mate. "I'm a good listener. That's all."

"Normally, I'm the one listening to people." She grinned but kept her gaze lowered. She exhaled. "Reality hit her hard on Sunday. Someone she loves is dying, and there is nothing she can do about it. The miracle we've been praying for isn't going to happen."

She raised her gaze to his. "She's lost everyone in her life, and when she loses this person… It's a tragic situation. Truly tragic."

She needs me. Michael needs to move out of the way and let me comfort her. Death is a part of life. Not even werewolves live forever, although we are damned near indestructible.

"I'm sorry," he said. *There is something else Zoe would tell me to say. Ah. Yes.* "You're a good friend to care so much."

"Aww. Thanks."

"So is it normal for a band to tour with a massage therapist?" he asked. *I don't know how I'm going to work on the road like that. She's going to have to change the way she schedules her business.*

"For Lainie, yes," she said. "For the rest of us, no. This is a huge opportunity for me."

"So, you're meeting the band? I heard from a reliable source"—he nodded to the girls—"that the lead singer is hot without any age qualifiers."

She laughed. Her shoulders dropped an inch. Her hands released their tight clasp and rested in her lap.

"Yeah, he's cute for a kid, and Lainie said he's

funny. She told me the drummer is the one who will decide if they take me as a replacement this year. I'm nervous." She moved closer to him. Her hands slid to the seat on either side of her thighs.

Lainie. Yes. Mine.

"You'll get the job." He pulled his hands onto his lap, signaling his lack of interest.

"So is this a second date for you?" Mere asked, smiling and doing an open-eyed don't-you-like-me-more-than-your-girlfriend thing before fluttering her lashes in an awkward flirting motion.

"Uh." *Back off, lady. I have a mate.* "She's a big fan and already has a ticket. She asked if I wanted to meet her because I came into town on business. I was going to surprise her with VIP tickets, but they were sold out. So, I bought one for an extravagant amount, hoping she might be *the one.*"

"We have an extra VIP pass for only you when she ignores you *if* you give us a ride back to the hotel and buy us dinner from the concessions?" Sara said.

"Sara Kilpatrick," her mother scolded her. "Stop negotiating everything."

"You've got yourself a businesswoman." He turned to Sara. "If you really have an extra pass to meet the band, you've got a deal."

"Deal." Sara stuck her hand out to shake on it.

"Deal." He shook her hand and turned to her mother, feigning a half smile. "That is, if you'll give up the extra pass to me." *Give it, or I'll take it.*

"I can't give it to you. You have to be with us to get backstage to meet the band," Mere said. "I was going to bring a local friend, but she sold her ticket an hour ago for nine hundred dollars.

A full, genuine grin spread over his lips. The fates were on his side.

"I think I may have bought that ticket. It's supposed to be at will call. The girl I'm meeting…" He weaved a tall tale that was hard to follow and left no room for questions about the fictional woman he expected to stand him up at the concert. Then he mentioned that he lived in Las Vegas and thought he might have met Lainie by accident in a nice hotel off The Strip, attempting to open the door for Mere to talk a little more. "I thought the massage therapist I met in Vegas was joking about traveling with high-profile clients. Could it be the same woman?"

"Lainie was in Vegas last week. She said she stayed in a great hotel with a funny name."

"The Midnight Howl Hotel?" he asked.

Mere nodded. "Yeah, that's the name."

"What a small world. I was rushing back to my room for my laptop. I literally bumped into her in the lobby. Her suitcase went flying. I barely caught her before she fell to the floor. Talk about awkward." He chuckled. "I apologized profusely as I helped her put her suitcase back together. She was extremely gracious. We chatted for a few minutes while she waited for her cab to the airport. It's got to be the same girl. Beautiful light-haired brunette with streaks of golden blonde and striking blue eyes?"

"That's, uh, her."

"I can't believe she's the band's therapist. Lainie Ivanovski is one mysterious girl."

"She sure is." Mere fidgeted in her seat, sliding a few inches away from him. "Mysterious and one of the nicest people you'll ever meet."

"My mom's single," Sara said, wiggling her eyebrows.

Mere sighed, flushing red. "Sara, stop it."

"What?" Sara asked, doe-eyed and openmouthed as if it were the most normal thing to say in the world. "He's single and hot for an old guy. You're single and superhot for a mom, and you're around the same age. Hot plus hot equals superhot. I'm just sayin'."

"You just want him to show up at your school to pick you up," Mere said. "Only, he's not from Georgia, and he's on a second date. So zip your lips, or I'll have Lainie watch you instead of letting you hang out with the *hot* lead singer, Eddie."

"Luke, I take it back. You're not hot, and you can't date my mom." Sara shook her head as she seemed to argue with herself. "I can't lie. You are hot. I don't want you to have self-esteem issues."

Kara handed him a piece of paper. "My mom's number."

"He's too big for your mom. But she is easy," Sara said.

Kara hit her in the arm. "She is not."

"Yes, she is," Sara said. "Guys don't care. At least that's what mom's last boyfriend said." She looked at him. "Am I right?"

He wasn't used to that kind of question from a stranger, but as with everything else in his life, he took on the role as Alpha and answered the question as he saw fit.

"Well, yeah, we do. Men like to conquer a challenge. If there is something really incredible between the man and woman. I'm talking about adults, not teenagers. Then things can kind of happen quickly. But making a man chase you shows the extent to which he's willing to go to be with you and also lets him know you're not available to just anyone."

The car stopped. With the engine idling, the driver stepped out of the car and opened their door.

The girls quickly climbed out.

"Thanks," Mere whispered as she slid out. "Sara's dad is kind of nonexistent, and she'll remember what you said."

Luke slid out behind Mere and led the way to will call to pick up his ticket and her VIP pass.

Once inside, he placed his hand at the small of Mere's back and guided her and the girls through the crowd, sniffing for his mate. *She's here.*

As they moved farther into the stadium, the crowds closed in on them. The girls walked closer and closer to him.

"I haven't been to a concert in forever." He hated unpredictable crowds, and concerts were filled with them.

The loud voices echoed off the concrete, irritating his ears. He needed earplugs to deafen the sound.

Sara grabbed his hand and curled her back into his chest.

He inhaled, catching the scent of fear radiating like uranium from the mother-and-daughter duo. Kara seemed the only one not on edge. He pulled Mere and Sara inside his protective arms.

"It's okay. I'm here," he whispered. *Nothing is going to happen to the humans my mate cares for.*

"Nothing to worry about."

"I didn't think it would be so packed." Mere trembled in his embrace.

"It's okay," he assured them. "Nobody can get through me."

Mere and Sara stopped and walked backward into him. The scent of fear burst from their pores like they'd been hit with a stink bomb.

"Shit," Mere mumbled. "Don't act like you see him, Sara." She glanced up at Luke. "Turn around. Get us to the seats another way, and I'll not only give you the VIP pass, but I'll have the band sign a guitar or something."

Kara gasped. She curled her arm around Luke's and tried to pull him in the opposite direction. "We need to go."

"Yeah," Mere whispered. "Now. Go. Now."

"You're safe," he said. *You're not with some fragile human.* He glanced ahead toward the entrance tunnel to their seats.

A large older teen wearing jeans hanging well under his ass and a designer red T-shirt glued to his chest stood alone near the restrooms watching them. His gaze seemed glued on Sara. The overgrown boy pushed away from the wall and grabbed his crotch. He sauntered toward them with a slow dip and quick rise with each step. He seemed to enjoy his size advantage the way he shoved people out of his way.

Luke stood his ground. *You have a lot to learn, kid. You're the prey in my world, not a predator.*

"Sara," the teen mumbled. His gaze lifted to Luke's, showing off the glassy haze of an addict.

Luke inhaled through his nose, pulling in the

boy's chemically altered scent and those he hung out with. A bully never went anywhere alone. Luke glanced to his left and his right, spotting three other older teens wearing similar clothing. He wanted to groan in misery for Sara as she shook in his arms. *Zoe and that damn sensitivity training seems to be rubbing off.*

The teen slouched and dropped his gaze to Sara again. His hands crossed at his dick, and he tugged up his jeans.

The mercurial behavior of an addict's response made any situation a challenge. The teen's gaze flitted from side to side. *Drugs got you paranoid?* His arm muscles twitched, and a sweat broke out over his pale skin. Luke sniffed. *An addict on the way down from a high. Won't be long before you need another fix.* Getting rid of the kid without too much of a scene might prove to be difficult. The scent of Jack and Ethan, the Alpha and Beta from the Arizona Werewolf Pack, caught his attention. The father-and-son duo ruled over a small and volatile pack of werewolves filled with a majority of males. The two handed down punishment swiftly and held the respect of Alphas around the world.

Ethan's scent is strong. He must have found his mate.

"Uh," Sara mumbled. Her body trembled, and her scent grew thick, expanding outward like a mate's.

Luke inhaled to confirm his suspicions. *Sara and Ethan. Shit. She's a compatible human.* Another human from Michael's territory was compatible with a wolf from his territory in the same century, in the same year, and the same month. *What is going on?*

"You need to leave," Luke said to the addict in front of him. He looked toward the concession stand, where Ethan's scent was strongest. *Son of a bitch.*

Jack and Ethan strode toward them like they were headed for war. *They will take care of the boy intimidating Sara. Ethan will show his worth to his mate.*

"Move over, old man," the boy said. "Sara's my girl."

Mere stepped in front of Sara. Her stance and attitude seemed suddenly strong, and the energy around her was fierce. "I have told you over and over. Leave. Sara. Alone."

"You want me to tell her your secret?"

Mere's hands clenched into fists. She widened her stance like a fighter. "Mind your own damned business, or I'll call the cops."

"Mom, it's okay. I can—"

Ethan pushed the bully out of the way and held out his hand to Mere. "Hi, I'm Ethan Ulvene. A friend of Luke's."

"Oh. Hey, I'm Meredith Kilpatrick." Mere's hands opened, and she shook his hand as if nothing was out of the ordinary. She seemed too comfortable adapting from a dangerous confrontation to a friendly one. Something was different about her. Mere stepped to the side. "This is—"

Kara scurried forward in front of Sara.

"I'm Kara." She bit her bottom lip and shimmied in front of him, preening like a peacock.

The boy glared at Sara. Jack smoothly transitioned to a fighting stance and stood between the teen and Ethan. Jack's soft voice held the calming tones of an Alpha trying to stop a fight. A security guard to the right of the tunnel ahead walked toward them and signaled to another guard. The kid swayed from side to side and reached into his pants pocket.

"Don't do it," Jack said.

Luke took two steps back with Sara safe in his arms. Ethan stepped forward and angled his body to block the situation behind him.

The kid jerked his hand from his pocket and aimed a gun at Jack.

"I warned you," Jack said and took control of the situation. He stepped forward and blocked Luke's view.

A sharp cracking of bone. Cries of misery exploded from the addict.

Jack forced the kid backward away from the group. He swiftly guided the kid to the ground and pinned him. Security descended on them.

Sara turned around in Luke's arms and wrapped her arms around his waist. "I don't want anyone hurt. He shouldn't be here. He won't leave me alone."

Luke held Sara as she continued to tremble. *You've got good instincts to stay with me. Soon, I'll be your Alpha.*

"It's okay," Luke whispered. "I'll protect you, and so will my friends."

The guards took over and hauled the kid away.

Security has the kid. It's all on tape. I gave them my business card to call me for a statement, Jack said through their mental werewolf connection. *I'm coming over to meet my son's beautiful mate.*

Great.

"Sara?" Ethan said. *May I take her, Alpha?* Ethan

asked.

There is no mating ceremony yet. Control your wolf.

Sara turned on a dime and stepped into Ethan's arms. She slipped her hands around his neck and quickly kissed his lips. "Thank you. Thank you. Thank you."

Ethan's pupils widened. His wolf peered out at Sara. "You're welcome," came from his mouth like a growl.

The new couple's mating scent strengthened, her peaches and pine to his cactus blooms and sand. The scents mixed and bonded.

Luke and Jack inhaled deeply.

Sara's face flushed. Her body was so aroused that Luke doubted she would last an hour before finding a private place with Ethan to have sex. They needed to have a werewolf witness the mating ceremony, and now wasn't the time.

Not in front of humans.

Luke would have to stop them, which was something unusual for him. He believed in allowing the mating to happen whenever and wherever the trance led them, but it had never happened around humans before. And Sara was young and human. She'd forever be eighteen while Ethan wouldn't stop aging until his beast was fully under control. Luke had to protect his kind and those who would become like him.

Jack strode to Mere and shook her hand. "I'm Jack, Ethan's dad. Is Sara's mom around?"

Meredith coughed. "Uh. I'm her mom."

Go with it, Jack.

"I see. Sorry. It's wonderful to meet you. Security has that kid..." Jack pulled Mere aside to speak with her privately.

"I was just about to get a drink. Do you want to come with me?" Ethan asked Sara, carefully sliding his fingertips between her flesh and the fabric of her jeans.

"Sure," Sara whispered. Her hips shifted from side to side. Her chest pressed against Ethan's. "I could go for a cola."

Jack and Mere rejoined the group but stood to the side. Mere's brows crinkled together, and her head tilted to the side as her gaze seemed to narrow in on Sara.

"Dad, Sara and I want to sit together. Maybe you could hang with Mr. Wolfson and his friends?" Ethan asked.

"Mom?" Sara pleaded.

Mere nodded.

Jack and Sara exchanged tickets as Kara drooled over Ethan's werewolf good looks.

Sorry, but Ethan's done playing with other girls. He found his mate.

Mating was mating. Once found, no one else would ever compare to Fate's pick. Mates never strayed, never divorced, and never left each other's side.

Except mine. Lainie, what is going on with you?

The heavy scent of mates preparing for the mating ceremony rushed through the area.

Luke grabbed Kara's hand as his gaze met Jack's.

Jack, protect the girls. Ethan is about to grow up fast.

I don't know if I can stop Ethan by myself, Jack said.

I've got it handled.

Luke walked Kara over to Mere and Jack for protection.

"I need a soda. Jack? Mere? Kara? Do you want a drink or something to eat? Anything?" *I have a mating to postpone.*

Mere reached into her purse as she asked for drinks and snacks, but Luke stopped her. "I've got it. Stay close to Jack. I'll meet you at the seats."

He walked off with his phone in his hand, already dialing the man he wasn't keen on talking to.

"What?" Michael answered.

"We've got a situation. A human from your territory and a wolf from mine are mates. I'm stopping them from starting the ceremony." He explained the situation, and for once, Michael didn't argue with his orders. "I'm holding off my young wolf, but mating is mating. There's only a short window before he loses control and takes her."

Luke hung up. *Shit. I fucking hung up on him. He's going to tell Zoe, and I'm going to have to spend the next hundred years in more of her dumbass sensitivity training seminars.*

He exhaled. *Doesn't matter. My mate is here. And tonight, I'm taking her home.*

He walked past the concession stand, finding the two lovebirds in an empty corridor a few feet away.

Sara moaned. Her back was flush against the cement wall and her legs wrapped around his waist. Ethan thrust and growled. Thrust and growled. Their mouths fused together in a heated kiss.

"She's eighteen," Luke said. "She'll always be this age."

"Yeah," Ethan panted. "Aware of that."

"You won't," Luke said, gearing up to postpone the inevitable. "You'll age."

Sara blushed, seemingly not comprehending any

of the conversation. "I'm not usually like this."

No fear radiated from her, only lust, and heavy doses of lust at that. It was the mating trance, not a mating heat, too—the double whammy Lainie had come to him in.

"Ethan's going to. Oh…" She unzipped his jeans.

"I've been waiting," Ethan whispered. "For you." He kissed her and moaned. "I need you. You smell so…"

The young man's eyes glazed over completely with the mating trance.

Her hands stroked Ethan's raging erection.

He brushed her cheek with his lips. "Please tell me you've never been with another guy."

"Never," she whispered.

"Stop torturing each other, and help me get drinks for everyone," Luke ordered.

They parted lips. But just barely.

Luke inspected her as though she was *his* child and frowned. Her shirt was askew and slightly ripped at the side seam. Her jeans were so low on her hips, they showed the little tuft of hair at the top of her lowered panties.

Her shoulder-length dark brown hair complemented her pale oval face and warm brown eyes. She had a nice figure. He and his beast approved of their mating. *She'll be a strong mate to Ethan and a solid member of his pack.*

"You need to understand Ethan is from Arizona, and you will live wherever he does," Luke said. "Are you willing to move to his home state?"

"Mom and I are moving to Tucson after I graduate in December. I'm going to massage school there," Sara said.

"No, we're together from this day forth. Wherever I am, you are."

As it should be. But for now, you'll have to wait. You're not fucking up my chance to see my mate again and bring her home.

"Drinks, kids," Luke said. "Almost time for the concert."

He grabbed Ethan by the shoulder and pulled him back as he wrapped Sara in his other arm and tugged her into his opposite side.

Sara gasped. "No."

"Yes." Luke growled. "You'll get time alone later. But for now you're stuck with me until this evening is over."

"Yes, sir," Ethan stood up straight and shoved his dick back in his jeans, his eyes clearing from the haze of the mating trance. "I'm sorry, Alpha."

"Help me with drinks," Luke whispered to him. "Control your beast. You'll only stop aging once you've gained control. If you take her today, she will not age another day, but you will grow old. Can you control your wolf? Can you force your wolf down when she starts begging for the mating? Show me you can. Show me you can wait."

"I'll try," Ethan whispered.

"Don't try. Do it."

CHAPTER SEVENTEEN

WITH THE HUMANS AND HIS pack mates accounted for, Luke allowed his wolf to rise closer to the surface. He and his wolf stared at the men onstage playing a love ballad for the crowd. He stood in front of his seat and swayed to the music in order to blend in with the humans around him. The singer and bass guitarist carried a light aroma of Lainie, but the drummer seemed to be bathed in Lainie's scent. The more the guy perspired, the more Lainie's scent called to him to take her. Luke's gums tingled.

Down, wolf. She touched him. He sniffed. *Jojoba oil. She massaged him.* His wolf receded slightly.

She should be with us, Luke's wolf said through their mental connection.

Tonight she will be.

Jack glanced around them. *Have you talked to your mate?* he asked through his mental werewolf link.

Things are more complicated than I expected. Luke answered.

I talked to my dad about it. His advice is to tread softly and listen to her, or your life will just get harder. Jack said through their link.

Luke nodded. *Thanks. It's good advice.*

He walked over to Ethan and Sara. The couples nearby parted for him to pass.

Ethan embraced Sara. Her back pressed against his front. His hips thrust forward as she pushed back. Her jeans were unzipped. His hands moved between her legs under her pants.

She moaned.

Luke stopped beside Ethan and spoke loudly into his ear. "Get your fingers out of her pussy. She's going to be your wife. You don't finger fuck her in public where there are phones and cameras available to record it. Do not disrespect your future mate." He coughed as the couple's overwhelming scent of sex and desire covered Lainie's aroma, interfering with his ability to track her. *Shit.*

Ethan's green eyes were almost too far gone.

Ethan, submit, Luke growled through their werewolf connection.

Ethan's eyes cleared from the haze. His gaze lowered. *Sorry, Alpha.*

"Hands out of her pants. And I know she's already orgasmed. So that should be enough for your wolf for an hour." *Had I been this out of it with Lainie?*

You're still out of it, Michael's voice whispered in his head. *You're not filtering your thoughts very well.*

Fuck you.

I'm trying to help you. She needs some more time, Michael added.

She needs me. Not. More. Time.

CHAPTER EIGHTEEN

LAINIE WAITED CLOSE TO THE door on the side of the long white table set up for signing autographs and taking pictures. The guys in the band sat behind the rectangular conference table covered in black linens as their adoring fans clamored for attention.

Michael and Gabriel stood behind her, guarding—always guarding—for any sign her beast was about to surface.

Where are you, Mere?

The VIP time was almost over. The line thinned. No Mere.

Don't flake out on me today. Please.

"She'll be here," Michael whispered.

"I sure hope so."

I can't leave until you get here. I need you to take over this tour. Damn it. Frank could be dying right now. He could be… She whimpered. *No. God, no. I want to go home.*

In only a few days, Frank's health had rapidly declined like Michael had predicted. He now stank of morphine, smoke, and chemicals. He'd never smelled so bad. He'd never looked so sick or so near death. She'd finally accepted the love of her life was not going to live out the month. The family she'd dreamed of having with him was just that. A dream that was dying with him.

She closed her eyes for a second, pulling her emotions back inside.

Lifting her lids, she searched the entrance.

The beautiful Mere Kilpatrick, her daughter Sara, and another teen girl walked through the door. A huge college boy and what looked like his father joined them. Then, *his* scent washed over her. *Mate.*

Her heart hammered. Her pussy trickled moist desire. Her breathing labored. *He came for me. He found a way. He tracked me. He wants me. He's going to take me.*

"Luke," she whispered. Her feet moved forward.

Michael swooped in, grabbed her wrist, and held her in place.

"Remember what Zoe said. She's our female historian. She knows more about our females than anyone on earth."

"I'll go furry quicker if I'm with him. I could change before the full moon. I could be a danger to those around me. I could lose control." Her voice lowered. "I could kill those I love."

She really wanted to cry, but she pasted on a miserable smile instead and ignored the overwhelming need to run into the arms of the man with the most beautiful green eyes she'd ever seen.

"Think about whiskey, peaches, and smoke to stay grounded in your humanity," Gabriel whispered, placing his arm around her back. "Under all the chemicals, Frank's scent is amazingly enticing."

She swallowed and nodded. *Dessert on our second date. Grilled peaches soaked in whiskey. The first time I ever made love to him, he tasted of aged whiskey and sweet Georgia peaches.*

"This is Sara and her friend Kara," Mere said, knocking her off memory lane. She bowed a little as she extended her hand with a flourish toward Luke. "And this is my savior tonight, Luke Wolfson. If it weren't for him, I'm not sure I'd be here right now."

"Not now," Michael said. He and Luke stared at each other like they were in a competition. Michael growled, but his gaze lowered first.

"Hi," Lainie said, ignoring Luke and the heavy pounding of his heart echoing in her ears as though it were radar guiding her closer and closer to him.

Luke growled low in his throat.

Her gaze flew to his. *Oh God, Luke. I can't. I can't. Please, stop. Please?*

"How did you meet Luke?" Lainie asked, trying to cool the fire flaming higher and higher inside her to get to her mate.

"Tonight, in the hotel lobby waiting in the line to catch a cab here," Mere said. "My friend decided to try and sell her ticket online. Luke ended up buying it. We drove over together, and he's really great." She leaned closer to Lainie. "If I thought I had a chance with him, I'd be flirting my ass off, but he didn't seem remotely interested even with Sara's bold teenager comments. I want to wash her mouth out with soap over a few of them."

Lainie laughed. "You're nervous?"

Mere slouched. "Whatever gave you that idea? Is it the incessant talking or the incessant talking?"

"You've got this," she assured her friend.

"Lainie," Luke said, holding out his hand. "I think we've met before."

Her gaze dropped to his enormous hand. *Strong. Powerful. Gentle. Loving.*

She placed her hand in his. Electricity sparked and flew through her system. The lights seemed to flicker around them.

She stepped forward, and she was in his arms, enveloped in his tantalizing scent and strength. *Need sex. Need you. Need. You.*

"Damn, you're glowing like you're the only one in white at cosmic bowling," Eddie said. "Dude, she's married. Stop trying to grope her."

The strong arms holding her lost their grip.

Eddie pulled her back.

"Not cool. She's all snuggly and shit, but she doesn't go for that. You're getting put on her blacklist. I'm on the record stating I didn't invite this guy."

"I'm okay. I know him," she said. The room seemed to spin around her. She couldn't see clearly. She couldn't focus. *Is this the trance?* "Um. Thanks."

"I've got your back," Eddie whispered. "I may act like I don't see what is happening to Frank, but I know. I'm not going to let you do something stupid because you're vulnerable. You've saved my ass from doing dumb shit too many times to count."

"Dang, you *are* glowing," Mere said. "What did you put on?"

"I want that," Sara said. "I've never seen anything like it."

Ethan growled. "You will. I'm going to make sure of it."

Lainie inhaled. *Peaches. Pine. Sand. What is that other scent? Mates. They're together. But she's like me. She's not. She hasn't. She's going to… Oh no.*

Luke's hand landed hard on Ethan's shoulder. "Not now."

"Hey, Luke," Michael said, moving between Sara and Ethan. "I didn't know you had VIP passes."

He shook Luke's hand, but it was not cordial. Each man's hand gripped the other's so tightly their knuckles turned white before Michael released his hold first. Her Georgia Alpha was pissed.

"I didn't. I ended up meeting Mere and the girls, who invited me backstage," Luke said.

"You okay?" Eddie asked as she watched Luke and Michael exchange words she couldn't hear.

She nodded. "Yeah. Luke's an old friend. I ran into him last week but lost his number. Thanks for asking." Her heart sank down, down, down. Guilt sledded down the blood rushing through her veins to her heart and burned a path of misery to her soul.

"He's more than an old friend. I won't say anything. I really can keep a secret." Eddie curled his arm around her waist, supporting her. "So, *Luke Wolfson*, what do you do?"

"Luke is most known for his golf course and country club designs, but he owns casinos and hotels too. He's got his hands in almost every type of business. He's a shark," Michael said. He put his arm around Luke and hugged him, which seemed more like a choke hold than a friendly embrace. "We go back a long, long way."

"Great. I can leave my girl with you, but no touching anything she hasn't uncovered," Eddie said.

"Ha-ha. No one is on the table, Eddie." Lainie rolled her eyes. "Mere's rules are the same as mine."

"Which one of the beautiful ladies is the highly recommended massage therapist Meredith Kilpatrick?"

Mere raised her hand like she was at roll call in elementary school. "That's me."

Eddie and the boys walked her and the girls out of the room, leaving Lainie and Luke in a Western-style standoff with the group of werewolves as spectators.

Chapter Nineteen

THE ROOM BUZZED WITH ENERGY. Lainie forced her feet to stay firmly in place. *Peaches. Whiskey. Smoke. Frank. Home.* Her lips trembled. Her chest constricted. *I have to stay strong. No turning.* Her hands drew into fists. *I'm going home.* She relaxed her grip and breathed deeply. *You're not touching me, Luke.*

As if he heard her and took it as a challenge, Luke moved fluidly like a stream avoiding a mountain around Michael and Gabriel to her. He enclosed her in his arms. Her world changed in his embrace. Time ceased to exist. Nothing mattered but him and his tantalizing scent.

"Mine," he whispered. "You're mine."

"Marigold, juniper, and sunshine." She lifted her gaze, finding his. "Luke."

"I love you," he whispered.

"You should have told me. You should have stopped it from happening. I hate you." Moisture wet her eyes. "You knew, and you still..." She shook her head as her body betrayed her human mind. She reached up and pulled his head toward her. "This isn't fair."

His hand on her back slid down, under her jeans, between her legs. "There is nothing anyone can do to stop the mating trance without a stronger Alpha to postpone it. No one is higher ranked than me except the World Alpha, and he wasn't there to stop it. You're mine. You don't hate me. You love me. You're coming home with me and divorcing your husband. I've waited three hundred and thirty-one years for you. No one is standing in my way. Not some human who means nothing to our future."

She coiled her arm and slapped him hard in the face. "Fuck you."

His eyes grew wide. His nostrils flared. His hand between her legs cupped her pussy while the other grabbed her wrists and pulled them behind her back.

"I intend to fuck you."

"Fuck you," she shouted.

"No, no, no, no. No. No." Michael's voice rose in a crescendo. "Luke. Stop."

Luke growled low and deep as though he was about to rip someone in two.

"You think you can fight. You haven't seen shit," she said quietly. "You haven't seen crazy. You haven't seen me lose control. Get your filthy paws off me, dog."

"Wolf." Luke's lids widened, and a smile spread over his lips. "I'm a wolf, Elaine. I'm your wolf. And I can't wait to see you get crazy, lose control. You're going to have to fight soon. You'll most likely have to get in the ring and fight the next highest-ranked female in our pack, and she's the second-best fighter in the world, behind only Zoe. Get crazy on her, and I'll reward you for it."

"I'm going to stake you through the heart." She twisted and turned in his arms, but he held firmly with just the right amount of pressure and give to restrain her without injury, pissing her off even more.

"That kills vampires, sweetheart," he cooed. "It only temporarily injures us. We get up and keep fighting."

"I'm going to cut your balls off." She jerked her head back and then forward to head butt him, but he tilted his head at the last second. She missed.

"It is almost impossible to cut them off without some specific torture devices. It's old-school, baby. No rules. No backing down. Lots of blood. It's not as satisfying as it might sound. They grow back." He licked his lips, and his lids dropped halfway down. "Damn, you're sexy all pissed off and aroused."

"I really hate you." She wiggled in his arms, but her center heated for him to keep going, to take her, and to make her submit because he deserved to have her.

"But I love you." He lifted her up against his chest and held her tightly.

She wrapped her legs around his narrow waist and leaned her head against his neck. "I'm not leaving with you."

With every breath, her body succumbed to his desires to make her submit. Her pussy clenched and ached to be filled with the hard rod pushing against her center. Her lips quivered to kiss his hungry mouth. *So. Close.*

Her tongue slid out and touched his bottom lip. She tasted him.

"Yes," he whispered.

Rip. Rip. Rip.

Cool air blew over her hot flesh.

Her bare back hit a cold wall. His bare cock pressed to her wet vagina.

"Oh. My. God," she whimpered as the man she needed right then pushed his long thick cock into her. All her reservations, her mores, and her thoughts of anyone but him left her. The mating trance sucked her in.

The room seemed to spin as pleasure assaulted her skin, her muscles, her bones, and her blood.

In and out, he thrust. Faster and faster. Pinned against the wall, he showed her the man who would continue to pursue her for the rest of his life, would love her, nurture her, protect her, and give her mind rest.

Her heart creaked, showing a weakness and a need to be healed. "Please, Luke."

More. More. More.

"Mine," he rumbled. His mouth dropped to her shoulder. "Mine."

She gasped as his teeth pierced her skin, delved into her muscle, and drove down through bone. The initial pain of the break morphed to elation, blissful rapture as his teeth and mouth locked into place.

Her gums tingled. Her teeth ached. Her nose itched. Her eyesight sharpened. A garbled noise came from her mouth.

In and out. In and out. Faster. Deeper. Her body vibrated with an increasing need to feel connected to him in a more substantial way, not just his body, but his soul.

His unrelenting cock demanded her full submission and her acceptance of his dominion over her. But she couldn't let him. He could have her body, but she had to stop from opening her heart and soul.

He dropped to his knees and took her with him. His body arched over her. His teeth clenched like a vise on her shoulder, marking her and staking his claim on her again. Her body was his. So much of her wanted to give in, give him the submission he demanded. More than part of her loved him. Needed him. But her mind woke up before she could give over her heart, exorcise her burdens, allow him to carry the heavy load slowly breaking her apart.

"Please, Luke…" *My husband is dying. I need to be with him. I have to be with him.*

I have to stop him. I have to get home.

Her teeth extended. Her jaw lengthened. Her body shook as the darkness inside her clawed to get out. The light in her soul dimmed as the powerful beast rose closer to the surface to take her mate, to claim him, to mark her territory, and to accept Alpha Luke Wolfson as her husband.

She slid her fingers along his neck to the strong beat of his carotid artery.

If she gave in to the dark desire to submit to him and let her beast out, she would have to leave with Luke and never see her husband again. If she refused to go with Luke once she turned, Zoe and Michael would keep her in quarantine until a solid link formed between her wolf and human brain, stopping her from ever seeing her husband alive again.

I can't morph into a wolf. I have to stop the beast from surfacing.

Mates go with mates under any and all circumstances, Zoe's voice whispered in her mind. *Your human life is over.*

Luke thrust and rotated his hips in a circle. He ground over her swollen clit.

The beast inside her growled, growing stronger and demanding freedom.

No. No. No. I'm not going to transform.

He rubbed back and forth over her hard nub. His cock tapped over and over against the sweetest of spots. She lost the battle, writhing under him and needing another shot of bliss to take her the rest of the way into his world. *So close. So close.*

The tight rope holding her heart together began unraveling. She couldn't let it. She shook her head. *No. I can't. I can't leave him.*

Her sensitive fingers palpated up and down along the beautiful muscle over the pulsing artery. *So healthy and strong. So physically powerful, like no man I've ever known.*

"*Grrrr.*" He mumbled a warning as if he knew what she was capable of when pushed into a corner.

With her body buzzing on the edge of a release, she pressed her fingers up under his jaw. She opened her mouth to warn him, but a long tongue rolled out. *No. I won't let you out.*

She curled her fingers into a fist. With every ounce of human strength she had left, she punched and pounded his head, neck, and shoulder.

I am not turning.

He held on. He wouldn't. Let. Go.

The more she fought, the stronger he seemed to become. *Alpha.*

Yes. He's your Alpha. Zoe's voice flowed into her thoughts. *He's the strongest Alpha in the world. He is smart and fierce. He's ambitious but diplomatic. He's loyal, faithful, and filled with integrity. Make the rest of your transformation. You're an eighth of the way there. Do it.*

Luke's hand slid under her ass. He rocked back and thrust forward. His thick finger slid into her dark passage.

A loud howling—hers—filled her ears as electricity rushed through her, building links and bonds and forming pictures of her and Luke, their wolves, and their baby surrounded by a golden glowing energy.

Hot spurts of liquid filled her as the sweetest bliss and the darkest misery broke her into a million pieces. Her wolf spirit soared to the heavens as her human soul sank into hell.

"I love you," he whispered. "This is the way it has to be."

"I'm going home to my husband," she whispered. "I didn't turn."

"You want to come with me."

"Yes, I do." She sighed. *Wait a minute.* "Damn it. No, I don't. You've got some kind of…" She gazed down at her shoulder where he had bitten her. "Why am I healed? I know you broke a few bones. It's tender, but what kind of—"

"We're still mating." He nuzzled her neck. "My claim is embedded into the marrow of your bones.

Into your very DNA."

His cock slid from her pussy as he licked a path from her neck to her breast.

She whimpered at the loss of him inside her.

"I need you." Moisture filled her eyes. "I don't want to need you."

"Mmm," he mumbled. He kissed his way down her torso, over her navel and mons to her center slit.

She lifted her knees to her chest, watching him and obeying his silent commands to submit to his desires.

He licked along the length of each side of her labia. Rubbed his nose at the junction of her thigh and hip.

"Pull apart your pussy lips," he ordered.

Lost in his touch, she caressed over her breast down the center of her body, slid her fingers between her labia, and spread them. "Like this?"

Brushing his cheeks up and down her entrance, he moaned. "Mine."

One long lick from her perineum to her clitoris made her want more. Another teasing lick. And another. She lifted her hips, needing more. So much more.

Two digits slid into her anus.

She squeaked as a third finger slid in. "Oh. My. God."

"Mine." His mouth covered her pussy, and a thick, long tongue dipped into her sheath.

In and out. His fingers. His tongue. His…

"Luke. I'm going to come. I'm going to come hard." Her hard little nub throbbed. "It's too much. Too much. Too good."

She bucked.

He lifted his head.

"Don't move." He dropped his mouth back into position.

Sharp teeth pushed into her tender pussy flesh.

"I'm already marked there. I'm already—" She gasped as a new sensation filled her pussy, a thin silver line of thread spilled forth from each sharp tooth, spun together, and extended, racing into her, heating her, and connecting her wolf to his. Her heart slammed against her chest with every pump of blood through her ventricles as the thread wove through her veins, making the darkness inside her take form, increasing its strength. "Luke." The sensation threatened to overwhelm her and take control.

Her vaginal walls contracted around his tongue. She had to do something to hold on to her life. She gazed at him.

His green eyes sparkled.

She reached down and grabbed a handful of hair.

He reached up and put his wrist at her mouth.

Her gums tingled. Her teeth lengthened.

He bit again. She bit.

Burning. Blood. Bliss.

Her jaw clenched. Her teeth buried into his flesh, easing the ache in her gums. The silver thread embedded deep. The link was thin but strong and permanent.

He pushed his wrist deeper into her mouth as he launched forward, his fingers slipping from her passage.

His hard cock found her entrance and tunneled into her.

"Yes," he shouted. "Fuck. Yes."

His rod probed her depths as her teeth crunched down, his bones giving way under her sharp canines. The delicious taste of his blood sliding down her throat. *Mine. Luke. Mine.*

"Yes." He withdrew from her pussy.

She released her hold. "More."

He crawled over her and placed his cock at her mouth.

His juniper, sunshine, and marigold scent, his body's strength, his growl, his magnificent power and beauty, his salty cum dripping onto her lips made her dark senses spring to life.

She opened her mouth.

His slick length inched past her lips. He twisted around. His balls dragged over her cheek and nose.

She sucked and swallowed.

"Yes," Luke said.

Hot breath and lips teased her pussy.

She sucked harder, taking more of his length down her throat. She swallowed over and over. His hips rose. His length retreated from her mouth.

Her chest rumbled.

His hips lowered as her tongue stroked his thick shaft. She sucked his length, took him deep, wouldn't let go until he smelled like her.

He nibbled her clit and her labia. His tongue fucked her. In and out. In and out.

Her gums ached. She needed to bite. She had to bite him. There was no other way. He was hers. *Mine. Mine. Mine.*

"Mine," he whispered.

She bit down into the flesh at the base of his cock as her pussy contracted in waves of ecstasy.

"Yes," Luke wailed.

Sweet blood and salty cum exploded in her mouth. Her teeth receded as she swallowed, sucked, swallowed, and sucked.

She closed her eyes and sighed as his cock left her mouth.

"Holy shit," Ethan gasped, knocking her out of the narrow tunnel she saw and heard through. "Is that normal?"

"This is on the extreme side," Michael whispered. "But Luke comes from our oldest pack, and their ways leave no room for questions about who belongs to whom."

"Will I do that? Wait, is that why he stopped me?" Ethan whispered. "I would have done that with Sara around humans?"

"You would have lost control with her around the humans. I don't know what you will do when you give in to the mating trance during the ceremony," Michael said. "That is why we have someone from the pack, usually the Alpha, witness the mating ceremony so it doesn't get out of control. You should be honored to have witnessed this portion of their mating."

She blinked several times as her brain seemed to work again. She met her mate's emerald eyes. "I didn't turn furry."

"No," he whispered. "You have incredible control. Allowing your teeth to extend while keeping your wolf from taking over is something learned over decades, and you already have that ability."

He cupped her face. His silver-sparkling wrist and forearm dotted with blood caught her attention.

She scrambled away from him. "I did that. Oh shit. I did that."

She glanced around the room, backing up against the black curtain covering the wall as Luke stalked after her.

"Yes, you did. It's normal. I'm not hurt. I'm healed. The blood is from the initial bite. That is all." He inched closer to her.

She lowered her chin.

"Don't look at yourself," Luke ordered.

She immediately dropped her gaze to her feet. Bloodstains on her ankles and toes, and now her ankles glowed. Her calves. Her thighs. Her pussy. The room spun. "No. Oh God. No."

The trance had made her human brain shut off during the heaviest parts of their mating.

I can't do this. I can't do this. Frank. Oh my God. Frank.

Her chest constricted. Heated perspiration popped up over her flesh. "Michael. I need to go home. Now."

"Yes. You're coming home with me." Luke's sexy voice seemed to float around her, kissing her and enticing her to drop to her knees and submit to each and every word.

Her legs weakened. But she shook her head.

"No. I'm going to my home, my husband, and my…" She stared up at him. "Michael, please. You told me I was yours. I live in your territory. I've accepted your rules and Zoe's too. You told me you'd allow me to…"

Her knees buckled under the weight of Luke's power blanketing the room.

"Stand back, Alpha Wolf," Zoe said. The clicking of her heels traveled from the left where she remembered Michael had stood. "I guess I got here just in time to stop a testosterone challenge."

A gentle hand stroked her hair. A folded pile of black clothes landed at her feet.

"Get dressed," Zoe demanded. "We'll deal with cleanup later."

Lainie's hand trembled as she dressed in front of everyone. She gazed up at the tall, slender blonde with an angel's face. "Please, Zoe, help me get home to my husband."

"Big dick over there has every right to take you wherever he wants. That is the world in which you now live. But I was charged with taking care of any human females who end up mated to a wolf." Zoe glanced over her shoulder and lifted her chin. "I'll get to you, Ethan, as soon as this matter is concluded. You better follow your daddy back to Arizona without the fragile human, or you're—"

"The fuck he will," Luke interrupted. "Mates are mates. They belong together. Don't get between him and his mate, or I will step in. He's under my rule. And in less than three weeks, his fragile human will be mine too."

"Oh my God, you are a badass," Lainie mumbled, not having meant to voice her thoughts aloud. "Shit." *My man doesn't back down to anyone.*

No, he doesn't, Michael said through their bond. *I can't stop him. I doubt anyone could.*

I can, Zoe added into their mental conversation.

Zoe's gaze drifted to Luke as she stepped in front of Lainie. "Well, Sara is mine and Michael's to deal with right now. We've got to prepare her for the transition. Ethan has to wait. I will be there for their mating to make sure it goes exactly as it should."

"If you're implying…" Luke's body tensed. "Step aside."

Zoe's feet moved to the side, lightning fast.

"Damn it." Zoe trembled, and her face crinkled with seemingly an incredible effort to stop her feet from continually increasing the distance from Lainie.

"You touch her again without my expressed permission, I will…" His arms enveloped Lainie. "Sweetheart, I love you. You're coming home with me."

She nodded. *The hell I am.*

"Give me a minute with Zoe in the bathroom, and I'll come back."

He smiled. "I'll get dressed."

Without thinking she kissed his lips. "I love you."

"I know this is hard," he whispered. "But everything is going to be all right."

The world she'd always known was crumbling down around her. He was wrong. Everything wasn't going to be all right. She'd done something so wrong by having sex with him, and she was being punished for it.

"Bathroom, please?"

"Okay, my love." He carefully placed her on her feet. "I'll be right here waiting for your return."

She nodded, catching Zoe's glare in the background.

She strode barefoot to the band's room with Zoe's heels clicking behind her.

"Hey, Lainie," Eddie said from the couch. "Mere is great. Benny and Clem have taken her and the girls back to the hotel. I thought I'd wait on you and Michael."

"Thanks. I'm going to my room to gather a few things and use the restroom."

"Great. Uh." His gaze rose over her to Zoe. His eyes bugged out, and a strange sweet-corn and sea-water scent filled the room. "Introduce me to your friend."

"Zoe Geroux, this is Eddie Chance."

He stood up, smiled, and leaped over the couch. He wrapped Zoe in his arms and dipped her back. "You're going to marry me."

"Shit," Zoe whispered. "Not today, hot stuff. I've got to—"

Eddie shut her up with a kiss Zoe seemed to return with as much zeal.

With Zoe distracted, Lainie hurried through the door to her room, grabbed her phone and purse, and ran as fast as she could out the private exit to her waiting car.

"Take me to my plane." She panted for air. "I have to get home quickly."

She called Frank's phone, hoping he would answer. She had to cover the house with security. Luke would get through, but she needed to make him go over a thousand obstacles first, or he would get there before her.

"Miss Lainie?" Curtis answered.

"It's me. I'm on my way to the plane. May I talk to Frank? Is he awake?"

"That's good, Miss Lainie. That's. Um." Curtis cleared his throat. "Good. Mr. Frank…" He swallowed over and over. "Mr. Frank." He sniffled and cleared his throat. "Hurry home. You were right.

You shouldn't have left this time. I shouldn't have forced you to get on that plane. I shouldn't have followed his orders. I shouldn't have lied for him. I'm so sorry."

All the air expelled from her lungs. The car seemed to tip over. She slumped in the seat.

"Hurry home," Curtis said. "He's barely holding on."

The phone slipped from her hand to the floor.

"You okay back there?" the driver asked.

"Get me to my plane." She gasped for more air. *Don't die, Frank. Don't die.*

CHAPTER TWENTY

ARRIVING BEFORE HER, LUKE STRODE with Michael by his side over the threshold of her mansion. The scent of death hung thick in the air. *Fuck.*

He coughed, nearly choking with every inhale of the foul scent. Yet, underneath the initial blast of decay, a male's tantalizing aroma of smoke, peaches, and whiskey lingered.

Smoke. My Lainie had a lingering scent of smoke on her. Peaches and whiskey. Her scent is inside the smoke. My mate bonded to a human like a werewolf.

Michael's hand landed on his shoulder.

"I don't know how this happened. Zoe's never heard of such a thing. It's not in our records. The World Alpha searched for any similar cases of a werewolf mating bond between humans. There are none. Zero. She's fully bonded to him, but she's fully bonded to you."

"We die if our mate dies," Luke said.

"That is usually the case, but Zoe confirmed some mates can survive. It's rare. Only one such case is recorded, but Lainie is an anomaly. And she has you."

Luke walked toward the miserable scent. "His kidneys are decayed. His liver… How is this guy still alive?"

"I think it has something to do with their strange bond," Michael said. "But I don't know."

The slow heartbeat of the man his mate chose before she met him stammered and stopped and stammered and stopped. Then slipped back into the sluggish beat of impending death.

The piercing sound of his mate's scream cut into his heart.

She blew past him like a tornado removing everything in its path.

His footsteps picked up speed as he followed her. *I have to hold her. I have to give her the strength she needs to survive. I should have listened to Michael. I should have come here to talk to her. I should have taken this week to comfort her and build our bond, not demand her return.*

Chemicals. Drugs. Death. He covered his nose. *The man should be long dead.*

She crawled into the human's bed and cuddled next to him.

"I love you. I'll always love you. There is no one else who will ever compare to you. No one."

A slight scent of whiskey and peaches lifted up from the putrefaction dominating the room. The man had minutes to live. The last of their extraordinary bond was dying along with him.

"Please move on, Lainie. Have babies. Fall in love. Michael is nice. You might not love him now, but give it some time. He's husband material. Father material. Curtis likes him too."

"Thanks, Frank," Michael said. "But I'm too boring for her."

The man's ashen lips curled slightly. "Lainie likes boring. She likes dogs. Did I tell you how she had a pack of dogs at her house when I first met her?"

"No," Michael said. "If you're up for telling it?"

"Who's your big friend?"

"I'm Luke Wolfson," he said, moving closer.

Lainie's arm curled around Frank's sunken chest, guarding him like a mate intent on protecting the last moments of love and then dying as soon as her mate passed on.

He swallowed a sense of panic. *I will help you survive his death. I will heal you. Our baby will heal you.*

"I'm a friend of Lainie's."

"More than a friend," Frank mumbled. "Your skin glows silver like hers. The light surrounding you is gold like hers." He closed his eyes and sighed. "Peaches and woods just like my Lainie."

Luke inhaled, focusing on breathing in her scent. "Tell me your story, Frank."

"Lainie grew up in rural southern Georgia. Her parents ran an organic chicken farm. My girl didn't care too much about the chickens."

"I loved the chickens. I just preferred to care for the dogs that got dumped on our property."

"Only they weren't dogs. They were injured wolves that liked to eat your chickens."

"Okay, Frank," she whispered. "They were mostly puppies."

Luke stepped to the edge of the bed and placed his hand on her back. *I'm here, Lainie. I'm sorry.*

"Those puppies grew up and moved with her to the big city. Only, there were six of them. Six gigantic black wolves in a one-bedroom apartment."

"Thank God she had them," Luke said. "Wolves protect their pack."

Frank coughed. Crimson blood stained his lips. "Yes, they do. The biggest one pushed me out the door and kicked it closed. Lainie opened the door and gave him a look. One look. He dropped to the floor and then rolled onto his belly. The others followed suit."

That's my mate. A leader. Strong. Fearless.

"Take care of her, Luke. Give her a child. Be the answer to my prayers. Be my miracle." He closed his lids. Droplets of tears fell from the corners of his eyes down his face. "I'll always be here with you, my love. In…" He inhaled sharply. "Your heart."

The death rattle rang like a bullhorn in his ears.

Lainie's entire body stiffened as she breathed in.

"No," she screamed, and the howl that followed nearly made Luke fall to his knees.

Her misery shattered his hardened veneer. His heart bled for her broken dreams. Their mate bond opened fully without any barriers. Images of her life with the man she had loved for the past eight years flooded his senses. Sex. Music. Massage. Friends. Triumphs. Defeats. Love permeated through it all.

For the first time in his entire three hundred and thirty-one years, he didn't know what to do or say.

The hospice nurse took off the monitor on Frank's finger and removed his IV line. "I'm sorry, Mrs. Ivanovski. He was a wonderful man."

The energy in the room shifted from sadness to fury. In less than a second, Michael grabbed the nurse and ran with her in his arms out of the bedroom. Lainie's clothes tore as her body expanded, her mouth lengthened, her bones shifted in seconds, breaking and reforming, yet she didn't cry or scream or tremble. Light brown fur sprouted like rows of soybeans on a farm over her flesh. She growled, showing her new fighting tools—claws and razor-sharp teeth.

"I'm here. You can guard him," he whispered. "No one is taking him away right now."

She stood over Frank's chest and glared at Luke as if he represented the enemy.

Her wolf guarded Frank's dead body as if the human still had a chance to come back from the dead.

Luke understood the instinct. He'd done the same as friends and family became casualties of war during centuries of fighting for ultimate power over the continents. Within the rage of a loved one's death, he'd found a will to survive and to keep fighting for life.

Please find the desire to live, for you, for me, and for our baby.

"I'll guard him too." He removed his clothes and placed them on the top of the dresser. He closed his eyes and accelerated the change, stretching his limbs, his neck, and his spine. Energy poured out of him. Bones broke, moved, and calcified. Black fur grew thick and long. He shook his body, and he opened his eyes. No one would enter the room. He turned his head toward her.

Slowly, she lowered down over her husband's body.

The blue of her eyes turned gray as if mist had

suddenly rolled in covering the beauty underneath. Her heart beat sluggishly as though the blood in her veins had turned to sludge. Her chest barely rose with each passing breath.

His heartbeat had a moment of an erratic rhythm. He had to get her to accept his bond over her dead husband's, or they were all going to die.

Come to me.

Inch by inch, she struggled to crawl to the end of the bed. Instinct kept him in place. She had to be strong to make it in his world. He had to be even stronger to protect her until she healed from the grief.

Time ticked on as she whimpered with each movement. Her brain seemed to turn off as her wolf took to saving them.

Her sweet face flopped off the end of the bed, panting.

You can do it, Lainie. You can make it.

Her hind legs found purchase against the metal rails of the bed and pushed. She fell off the bed, but he caught her, grabbing her at the back of the neck with his mouth and carrying the small wolf to the bedroom door. He gently laid her down and stood over her.

You're mine to protect, to nurture, and to love.

Her heartbeat increased. Her breathing evened out as she fell asleep beneath him.

She's strong, Michael said through their pack link.

Start the preparations for his funeral. She's coming home with me immediately after the burial.

CHAPTER TWENTY-ONE

A STEADY SPRINKLING OF RAIN FELL from the gray sky as Luke watched her stand alone at the edge of the open grave, staring down at the wooden casket. So many friends had been there, paid their respects, and left, but a small group of humans stayed under the dry green tent watching her silently cry.

Waiting patiently at the back of the tent with his Beta, Danny Wedekind, Luke listened through their bond for her inner voice to call for him but heard nothing. Nothing but heartbreak.

He pushed through her misery, calling for her to say something. But the thick silver cables wrapped around the thin thread linking their lives didn't seem strong enough to hold her together *and* communicate. Her wolf had retreated into the depths of her soul to rest, recuperate, and grow while the human part of her went through the motions of mourning.

Keeping his distance from his ailing mate became a test of will. He wouldn't disrespect her relationship with the man. Not when the world watched her and spied on her interactions with every man who gave his condolences. Pictures of her with her husband had been plastered everywhere over the past few days.

Danny's hand landed on his shoulder. "Chrissy Clemmons called. She's not challenging Lainie to fight. She made it public. Seems your mate has the respect of our women worldwide."

He nodded. *Mates die together. My mate survived. She would destroy Chrissy. Not even Zoe is stronger than my beautiful mate.*

Danny squeezed his shoulder. "How much longer before you go and get her?"

"She lost her mate and lived. She can stay beside his grave and mourn him for as long as she needs to."

She turned around. She was soaked to the bone, her black dress clinging to her skin and her hair falling in wet, wavy strings framing her face. She walked away from the grave like she would collapse at any moment, but she didn't. She stopped under the tent.

Luke, I need you, she whispered through their bond.

He moved quickly, wasting no time getting to her side. He tucked her under his arm. *I'm here. I've got you.*

"Thank you for staying," she said. "I'm…" She trembled. "He. Frank."

A tall redhead in a green dress stepped forward and closed her hand around Lainie's.

"The single released today. His voice. The lyrics he wrote. No wonder you were so protective of your life. Love like that"—the woman paused and shook her head—"is what we all dream of having."

Lainie nodded.

The woman hugged her, whispering, "I'm so sorry about the way I acted. I'm embarrassed. Please forgive me."

"Forgiven," his mate whispered. "Ginger, thank you for coming today."

"If you ever need anything now or in the future, all you need to do is ask me. Stand strong. I've got your back, and I'm good with a whip." She patted Lainie's ass and stepped back. "Always wanted to do that."

His mate shook her head and laughed even with her lips quivering. "You're never going to keep a good massage therapist."

"I'll wait for you," the sassy woman said. "No one can hold a candle to you." She strutted from the tent, opening a red umbrella as she stepped into the rain.

He stood holding her, guarding her as the others quickly came forward, chatted for a minute, and exited.

"Ready?" he asked.

She nodded.

He walked at her pace to the car.

Danny opened the back door for them.

She stepped into the car. "Thank you, Danny."

"You're welcome," he answered.

Luke joined her in the back and shut the door.

His beautiful mate's head hung low, her long hair a sopping wet mess. He grabbed the blankets he had brought and swaddled her. He pulled her into his lap and held her as the car rolled forward. He kissed her forehead and brushed his cheek against hers.

"I love you," he whispered.

She rested her head in the crook of his arm, silent. He looked down at her.

Her gaze rose to his for the first time since the night Frank died. "I don't want to leave my home. Please don't make me."

Sad blue eyes held a glimmer of life in them.

"We're headed to the airport now."

"I'm not ready." Her pulse quickened. He inhaled. Peaches. Peanuts. Pine. Sunshine. Marigold. Juniper with barely a hint of whiskey.

He'd never been so unsure of making a decision in his life.

Pushing her to move to Nevada immediately would build their bond. The pack would quickly fill her days with events, lunches, clubs, parties, and get her focused on life instead of death. Yet the transition would be radically different, possibly too much for her to process.

"No," she shook her head.

Her cheeks flushed pink. She crossed her legs under the blankets.

He leaned forward with his lips almost touching hers.

Heavy puffs of sweet sexy air blew from her mouth. "No, Luke."

He cradled the back of her head as his instincts called for him to listen to her needs. "One day. We leave tomorrow."

"Thank you," she whispered. "Thank you."

Chapter Twenty-Two

AS HE SLEPT BESIDE HER in the guest room of her home in Georgia, she watched the leisurely rise and fall of his chest, and her overactive mind calmed. With her palm flat over his sternum, she felt the strong, steady beat of his heart pumping life through his veins. Every beat of his heart gave her a reason to keep going, keep breathing, and keep pushing against the overwhelming sadness she constantly battled. Leaving her home wasn't an option. Not until she could get out of bed and face an unknown future. Accepting the last requests of her late husband seemed a daunting task. *Move on. Fall in love. Have children. Have a family. Live and love for both of them.*

In the darkest days of despair, Luke had lifted her hand to his heart, promising her a life filled with health, family, and love. While she slept, he appeared in her dreams, chasing away the grief calling her to the grave. His presence brought her the light of the sun, showing a destiny much bigger than she'd ever imagined.

He stayed in Georgia, taking care of her for

weeks while the deepest wounds of her lost bond with Frank scarred over. He never left her side and postponed the ceremony for his promotion as Alpha over all the American continents until she could survive traveling to Nevada.

The silver thread of their mating bond thickened, grew, expanded with each passing day, exactly like he said it would. Yet, the miracle of life she carried inside her remained silent, the scent of his or her presence hidden. The bond between mother and child was invisible.

Sliding her leg over his, she snuggled closer, rested her head on his chest, and caressed along the massive muscles across his rib cage to his side. *Three hundred thirty-one years old and perfectly healthy.*

He squeezed her bare ass.

"Mine," he mumbled.

Her wolf awakened with a sexy growl. Her body heated, and the desire that lay dormant for weeks burst to life.

Two thick fingers slid between her folds into her pussy.

Accepting and encouraging his intimate touch, she rolled her hips, pushing his fingers deeper, dipping into a sweet spot.

She moaned.

A heavy rumble vibrated his chest.

He rolled over, taking her with him until he held her under his powerful body. His firm grip on her ass drove his long digits farther up her channel, lighting up another lovely spot. He curled the tips of his fingers, stroking along the most sensitive parts of her pussy.

"Wolf?" His chest expanded with an inhale.

"Lainie?"

Sensing his uncertainty, she raised her gaze to the vibrant green eyes questioning which part of her called to him—wolf or human. "It's Lainie."

His fingers retreated. His pelvis dropped, pushing his cock against her sex.

Keeping eye contact, she wrapped her legs around his waist. She slid her arms up his chest until the tips of her fingers touched the wooden headboard and surrendered to his authority.

His pupils widened as the green of his irises began to sparkle with the sign of his wolf surfacing. Slowly the irises shrank to thin circles of sparkling emerald green showing her his beast's approving eyes.

Peace, contentment, and a hungry need to have him pulsed through her and her wolf.

"You're connected to your wolf," he whispered. "She's grown. Barely recognizable as a pup."

A Southern drawl-like growl escaped from her lips. "What's inside me has a mind of her own."

He smiled. His irises widened, and his pupils shrank with his wolf's retreat. "Not for long."

He slid his right hand from under her ass upward, massaging in leisurely circles along either side of her spine to the back of her neck. He dropped down on his right elbow. He reached forward with his left hand and clasped her wrist tightly.

He thrust his hips forward, driving his hard cock past her pussy lips and deep into her channel.

She moaned. Her pussy rippled in waves of pleasure, squeezing his thick cock.

New sensations traveled through her flesh, originating from the mating marks Luke had given her.

A different bond formed from the original, connecting each mark to the other as it traversed her skin, finding new ways to penetrate into her system. The fresh bond permeated her flesh, searching to form deeper and more powerful links to her wolf and Luke's lifeline. Thin silver threads morphed into thick, sparkling titanium spindles and spun into the abyss of her soul's wound left from Frank's death.

Like a spider's web, the spindles wove around her bones and muscles, cutting and filling the holes with something altogether magical and strange. The pattern spiraled, crossed, and twisted as they grew thicker and stronger as if chainmail armor raced through her system until it covered every inch of her body inside and out.

In a surge of energy, thousands of glittery silver strands burst from her mating marks, extending through the air, and covered Luke. The sparkling silver vanished as it absorbed into his skin, but the energy buzzed like electricity between them.

Her lungs expanded, breathing in his delicious scent along with the cumulative aromas of the community of wolves he ruled over. Her eyesight sharpened, seeing colors and tones in variances previously unknown. Her hearing amplified, allowing her to listen to animals, and conversations far from her location.

Frank's dying words whispered in her mind. *"Live and love for both of us."*

Luke rolled to his side and pulled her against his chest. "There's no pressure. Let the bond settle in. This is all new to you."

"I don't understand what just happened. I

thought we were already bonded."

"We were. We are. It expands and strengthens as we go through trials in life. Your wolf is gaining power, growing larger, getting ready to emerge again. You can travel now."

"No. I'm not ready." She shut her eyes. "Please, just a few more weeks."

He sighed.

"Please, Luke?"

"No."

She wiggled out of his hold, scrambled off the bed, and supernaturally fast, she fled to her husband's music studio with Luke following a short distance behind her.

She slammed the door shut in his face.

"Got you out of bed, beautiful."

"Go away."

"See, you're up for having a little separation." He chuckled.

Her blood boiled. "I'm going to punch you in the junk if you even think about coming in here."

"I'll survive." His elation pushed through their bond, infuriating her more.

Huffing and stomping, she strode around the perfectly maintained music studio and stopped outside the sound room. She peered through the glass. Beyond the grand piano situated at the right center of the room, Frank's favorite guitars stood like soldiers at attention lined up in stands along the side and back walls. A small white envelope with her name on it was woven through the neck strings. His MP3 player and earphones hung on a hook above it.

"Why couldn't there be a cure for you? Why did

you have to die?"

The *whoosh* of air alerted her to the door opening. Luke's scent immediately filled the room.

Without thinking, she opened the door to the sound room.

Hurrying inside to avoid her big, bad wolf, she closed the door behind her and sucked in the peaches, smoke, and whiskey aroma of Frank's life.

"Lainie, don't do this to yourself. Please, stop finding ways to slip back into misery."

She strode to the acoustic guitar he bought on their excursion to Memphis, Tennessee, the first year they were married.

Her hands held steady, slipping the note from the strings, as her insides quaked.

"I'm coming in," Luke said, his voice seemed lost in uncertainty.

"No. Stay there." She opened the envelope and took out the note with his monogram on the front.

Lainie,

You've had more than your share of heartbreak, and I'm sorry I'm now a part of that. But a miracle is coming for you. When my miracle comes along, and I know it will, don't fight it. Fall into it.

Put on the headphones. Press Play.

Forever in your heart,

Frank

Her composure cracked as she tried to slide the note back into its envelope.

Both pieces fell to the floor.

Desperate to hear his voice, she removed the devices from the hook. Her hands trembled as she fitted the headphones over her head. She held the MP3 player to her heart and pressed Play.

"Fall into Love," Frank whispered. "I love you, Lainie Ivanovski."

"Ready, Frank?" Dirty Dog's tenor voice whispered into her ear.

She sank to the floor and sat cross-legged as Frank cleared his throat.

"Ready," Frank said.

The familiar strumming of the Frank's favorite guitar transported her back in time to the private moments when he would write music and sing to her.

"Listen to my words, my true love.
When my miracle comes,
And I know it will.
My love is coming to save you." Frank sang the words as the rhythm of the music slowed, accommodating Frank's weak voice and shallow breaths.

"I sent you away to find someone new.
You came back lost. Confused." Frank coughed, but the music continued.

"When my miracle comes." Dirty Dog's voice took over as Frank fought to breathe. The beautiful thrumming of the guitar stopped, but Frank's friend continued singing. *"When my mir-a-cle..."* His voice cracked. *"Comes. And I pray it does. It's my love coming to save you."*

She rocked back and forth, gripping the device against her chest, needing him with her, not stuck six feet underground. Frank's voice took over and began singing again.

"When my miracle comes,
And I pray it does.
My love will grow inside you." His struggling breaths broke her down. His voice betrayed the

tears she heard him try to hide.

"When my miracle comes,

And I pray it does." His desperate sobs for her to believe in miracles thundered in her ears.

The storm of loss always on the cusp of exploding inside her soul raged loudly against the fragility of life. The truth of Luke's words finally sank in. *Human life is fragile. They die easily.*

Frank's shaky voice continued on.

"His love will sustain you

Like yours sustained me

When I found out I would lose everything." His voice faltered. *"Fall into love.*

For just one night.

Fall into love.

For the rest of your life.

Fall into love, Lainie,

For the rest of your life." His breathing slowed. He swallowed.

The soft strum of the guitar played in the background as the faint sound of Dirty Dog's soulful voice sang more of the lyrics under the inhalations of the man she'd lost.

"When my miracle comes,

And I pray he does,

Fall into his love…"

"Lainie," Luke called.

She looked over her shoulder. Luke pushed the door to the room open.

Frank whispered, "When my miracle comes. And I pray he does. Fall into his love. For just one night. Fall into his love, Lainie, for the rest of your life."

She rose on shaky legs and ran to Luke, falling into his open arms.

Tucked in his loving embrace, she listened to the rest of the song. The connection she'd lost in Frank's death found a new pathway into her soul through his music.

Luke gently removed her headphones and took the player clasped at her heart from her hand.

"I was worried," he whispered as she wrapped her arms around his waist. "But you seem better now."

She nodded. She was unable to speak with the flux of emotions trapped in her throat.

"I love you," he said. "I love you."

"I love you too," she whispered.

She gazed up into his eyes. "Can we bring his guitars? His piano? All his music?"

"Yes, sweetheart. Whatever you need."

She nodded and snuggled back into his embrace. *I'm getting there, Luke. I'm getting there. Just a little more time. Please.*

He held her, not answering. He blocked her from his thoughts and feelings.

"We'll see," he whispered.

CHAPTER TWENTY-THREE

L UKE'S NOSTRILS FLARED FOR THE thousandth time in the past hour. With his shirt long gone, his broad bare chest seemed to expand and bulge with more and more muscles as he carefully removed each piece of furniture she'd pushed as a barrier between them. His freaking ten-pack abs rippled in waves with each heavy breath. The low-riding jeans hugged and bagged in all the right places as he picked up another piece of furniture obstructing his ability to get to her.

"I'm not leaving," she said. At some point he would get to her, but it was going to take him a little while.

"Yes, you are." He lifted Frank's large mahogany desk up as if it was a child's small toy and carried it out the French doors to the sunroom. "Mates stay with mates."

She rose on the balls of her feet on top of the king-size bed Luke had bought and peered over the filing cabinet to see him return.

He walked back in with a bottle of water. He poured it over his head and chest.

She rubbed her lips together. "You missed a spot."

"Really?" His left brow rose.

"Uh-huh." She nodded and pointed to his groin.

He unbuttoned his jeans and lowered the zipper, uncovering his erection.

She licked her lips as her gaze followed the movement of his hands along his smooth cock.

"Yeah, I missed this area." He caressed down over his denim-covered thighs.

She swallowed the saliva that was building up in her mouth. *Drool worthy.*

"Thanks." He zipped up his pants. He shoved the couch, armoire, the rolled-up area rugs, and two bookcases to the side. He stood on the other side of the filing cabinet, the last obstacle he had to hurdle to get to her.

She stepped down off the mattress and looked around for something else to block his entrance.

He leaped over the six-foot-tall cabinet, landed behind her, and firmly gripped her hips.

"We are leaving now."

So much of her wanted to leave with him, but her heart was here at home. Her life and business was here. *I can't leave.*

"Can't you just go, and when the separation becomes too much, come back?"

"No." He ended the negotiations, using the big boy Alpha voice that had sent Zoe away weeks ago.

She leaned back against his front. "No need to go Alpha Commander on me."

"I've given you five weeks. No more." He twirled her around and threw her over his shoulder.

"I miss him," she whispered.

"I know." He carried her out of the bedroom

through the French doors into the sunroom.

"I'm sorry, Luke."

"I know. I'm sorry too." He set her down on her feet on the travertine-tiled floor, facing him. "Do you want to come with me?"

She nodded.

"I shouldn't, but I do. I'm scared. Listening to his music helps, but my heart aches when I leave the house. I don't know what else to do. I don't want to die. I don't want you to die. I don't want our baby to die."

"No one is going to die."

"But that fight-to-the-death thing. I might not make it. I—"

"No one wants to fight you," he whispered. "Not one female has stepped forward. Someone has to challenge you for there to be a fight. The one person I assumed would come forth has officially said she will not challenge you. I don't anticipate there will be any other takers. I'll still train you for the possibility, but it's not going to happen."

He led her through rooms to the front of the house and helped her into the back of the white SUV idling in the driveway with Danny at the wheel.

He climbed in next to her.

She closed her eyes and opened the bond between them. *My heart isn't a pretty place sometimes.*

I have three hundred plus years of baggage. Whatever you're worried about me seeing pales in comparison to what I've actually done.

"Tell me you haven't slept with thousands of women."

"Thousands? No."

Her hands drew into fists. She did not like his answer, and neither did her wolf. "We're going to have some rules set up for you."

He chuckled and pulled her into his lap. "I'm the Alpha. I make the rules."

She snuggled into his comforting hold. "Tell me about your rules, Mr. Wolfson."

"Well, they start with you agreeing to have sex whenever and wherever I want."

"Not in front of people," she said.

"Rule number two. You agree to allow the pack females to pamper you."

"Pampering? How?"

"Rule number three. You will bare your belly at all times while on our property."

"What kind of rules are these?"

"Rule number four. You will obey all my commands."

She huffed. "You're not serious."

"Number five. You will tell our baby you love him or her every day." His voice softened. "You do love our baby, don't you?"

"I love our baby." She lifted her gaze to his worried eyes. "I love you too. It scares me how much I need you."

The right corner of his mouth drew up into a lopsided smile. "Rule number six. You will wear dresses and skirts. No jeans, pants, or shorts."

She barked a laugh. "Kiss my ass. I'm a massage therapist. I wear jeans to work. I'm not baring my midriff for my clients or the wolf pack. Give me a break." She rolled her eyes and snuggled down against his chest. "You're just trying to distract me."

"Rule number six is now amended. You will

wear appropriate clothes while working as a massage therapist with everyone but me."

"Thank you."

"Rule number seven."

"You can stop now." She slid her hand over her belly. *I love you. I love your father. I may tease and play, but your father is perfect.*

Her lips and chin trembled. Her eyes filled with tears as the ache for Frank and her home returned. *Your father is the strongest man I've ever met. He's kind and loving. He's handsome and brilliant. He knows just what to say and do to help me through my grief. Don't tell him I'm telling you this, but…* She looked up into Luke's eyes. *I accept him as my Alpha, and before you're born—if he ever asks—I hope he'll be my husband.*

He cradled the back of her head in his palm. "The werewolf world heard you."

She relaxed as he dipped her back and pressed a sweet kiss to her lips.

"It's all true."

The End

Titles by Anna Lores

Paranormal Romance

One Night of Love
Cursed to Love

Contemporary Romance

Ella's Triple Pleasure
The Horse List
The Horse List Challenge
The Horse List Unveiled

For more steamy stories, visit Anna at
www.AnnaLoresAuthor.com

About Anna Lores

An avid romance reader, Anna Lores started writing steamy romance novels as a by-product of insomnia. One night, with a nudge from her husband to write a book, Anna borrowed her son's laptop and set about breathing life to her very own characters. After a month, she was surprised with a new laptop of her own to pursue her dreams of writing sensual happily ever afters.

The desire to fill her world with wonderful stories she and her close friends could not just talk about but gush over keeps Anna's fingers racing to keep up with her imagination. As the rest of the house is sleeping peacefully, Anna sheds her title as Supermom of Three to write sexy love stories

Sleeping might still be a battle Anna hasn't conquered, but armed with a B.A. in English Literature and all the hot men in her mind calling for their own story, she stays busy during those midnight hours writing her next international bestselling spicy romance.

Visit *www.AnnaLoresAuthor.com* for more information and to sign up for Anna's VIP Newsletter.